AFTER THE ROADS

Sidney's Way volume 1

a Five Roads to Texas novel

Written by
BRIAN PARKER

Edited by
AURORA DEWATER

Illustrated by
AJ POWERS

DISCLAIMER

This is a work of fiction. Names, characters, places and incidents are the product of the author's imagination and are used fictitiously. Any resemblance to actual events, locales, or persons, living or dead, is purely coincidental.

Notice: The views expressed herein are NOT endorsed by the United States Government, Department of Defense or Department of the Army.

COPYRIGHT

AFTER THE ROADS

Copyright © 2018 by Brian Parker
All rights reserved. Published by Phalanx Press.
www.PhalanxPress.com

This book is protected under the copyright laws of the United States of America. Any reproduction or other unauthorized use of the material or artwork herein is prohibited without the express written permission of the author.

Five Roads to Texas: a Phalanx Press Collaboration

Haven't read the start of Sidney's journey yet? Get your copy on Amazon.

Works available by Brian Parker

Easytown Novels
The Immorality Clause
Tears of a Clone
West End Droids & East End Dames
High Tech/Low Life: An Easytown Anthology

The Path of Ashes
A Path of Ashes
Fireside
Dark Embers

Washington, Dead City
GNASH
REND
SEVER

Stand Alone Works
Grudge
Enduring Armageddon
Origins of the Outbreak
The Collective Protocol
Battle Damage Assessment
Zombie in the Basement
Self-Publishing the Hard Way

Plus, many more anthology contributions and short stories

Only the dead have seen the end of war.
~ George Santayana

PROLOGUE

Death.

Today was the same as yesterday. Yesterday was the same as the day before that. For the soldiers of Able Company, there was no point in keeping track of the days of the week. The men and women didn't mark the days off on a calendar. There was no going home at the end of their deployment. This was their life.

This was America.

Lieutenant Jake Murphy sighed as he wiped ash away from the lens of his ACOG scope. He lifted the rifle up to his shoulder and pressed his cheek against the plastic stock, lining up the small red dot of his optics on the twisted, bloody face of an infected. It was a woman. Her exposed torso was thin and muscular. Scratches, bruises, and streaks of dried blood did little to conceal her nakedness. Jake supposed she'd been pretty at one time, but now her face was twisted in rage as she screamed her hatred at the non-infected soldiers on the wall.

The soldiers, elevated nearly thirty feet above their targets, protected the millions of refugees who'd sought sanctuary inside Fort Bliss when the FEMA camps outside the base were inevitably overrun. The camps, with their chain link and barbed wire fences, had been no match for the hordes of infected that made their way across the desert sands, chasing their quarry toward the so-called "Safe Zone."

He supposed the Army knew the camps would fail, which is why they'd created the perimeter wall from thousands of forty-foot shipping containers, stacked end-to-end and two high. It gave them excellent fields of fire from above against their enemy, an unthinking, untiring, unstoppable mass of humanity.

A wave of heat and light washed over the lieutenant, causing him to momentarily break his cheek-to-stock pressure. His men were lighting the bodies below, simultaneously burning the dead and living alike. The fires, while terrible and sickening, were an absolute necessity. Otherwise the infected would be able to swarm over the mounds of their brethren and overrun the base.

He rested his cheek against the weapon once again, but peered over the top of the scope with his naked eye to reacquire his target. There she was; the blonde with the lithe, muscular body. He raised the barrel slightly to bring the ACOG into his line of sight. Magnified now, he led her slightly as she jogged doggedly toward the wall, allowing himself a moment to wonder what she'd been before the infection took her. Had she been a dancer, or a student? Maybe she'd been a mother, or even a soldier like him.

Whatever she'd been, it didn't matter now. His aim didn't waiver as she crossed behind the red dot in his scope. He squeezed the trigger.

The round was lower than he'd wanted, it took her through the neck, snapping her spine and dropping her instantly. She'd lay there until she bled out and died.

Jake made a mental adjustment to his aimpoint as he elevated the barrel of his M-4 to find a new target while the Stryker behind him engaged targets at a greater distance.

Boredom.

Today was the same as yesterday. Yesterday was the same as the day before that. For the refugees trapped in the confines of Fort Bliss, Texas there was no point in keeping track of the days of the week. The men and women didn't mark the days off on a calendar. There was no going home at the end of their stay. This was their life.

This was America.

Sidney exhaled forcefully as she attempted to button her pants unsuccessfully. It was no use, she was only about six months along but she'd been so thin before the pregnancy that her stomach had more than doubled in size. There was no way she was going to get her pants to button.

She looked around her tent for something to help her out. The tent was the most expensive one available at REI that day she'd rushed to the store and grabbed all of her and Lincoln's supplies after they first heard the news of the pending nationwide outbreak of madness. Not being a hiker or camper, she hadn't known if the tent was the best one on the market or simply some type of designer brand, but it had held up well, even in the heavy rains of late spring and the wind storms of early fall.

The blow-up mattress was another last-minute grab from Lincoln's house, something left over from his college days. She'd had to trade some of her precious canned goods for a bicycle pump once she made it to the camp, though. There was no way she'd be able to continue to find six D batteries each time the damn thing deflated.

Knives, first aid kits, Linc's clothes… She let out a quick huff and opened his pack that sat in the corner, mostly undisturbed. Inside, she found a few pairs of shorts, several t-shirts, and one pair of jeans. For such a smart guy, he sure as hell hadn't thought a lot about the everyday stuff. She remembered him telling her that they'd be able to get clothes in the Safe Zone, so he traded the space in his bag for more food. It was a good call at the time, but now that she was actually here, there were no clothes to be had. Supplies were limited, and there was never enough of anything to go around.

The camp designers hadn't expected the FEMA camps to fall. The small section of the larger base that she occupied, Fort Bliss Refugee Camp #3, was originally designed for 150,000 people max. Today, there were over four hundred thousand in the camp, and *millions* more cramped behind the walls, cowering in fear while the military defended them. Food, ammunition, clothing, *patience*—all were stretched to the breaking point. How much longer could they hold out?

She pulled her pants off and groaned as the fine layer of hair on her legs scraped along the material. Razor blades were another luxury commodity that had ran out quickly. Now, almost all the men sported beards and women had lovely, flowing carpets of fur sprouting from everywhere.

Surprisingly, Lincoln's jeans fit okay. They were much too long for her, so she cuffed the ankles, but they fit her waist, which was the most important part. If the baby continued to grow as rapidly as it had been, his pants would only buy her a few more weeks at the most. Then she would be in trouble.

As the resident camp pariah, she didn't have the option to trade with anyone in her immediate blocks. She'd have to start searching farther out.

1

SURVIVOR CAMP #3, EL PASO, TEXAS
SEPTEMBER 14TH

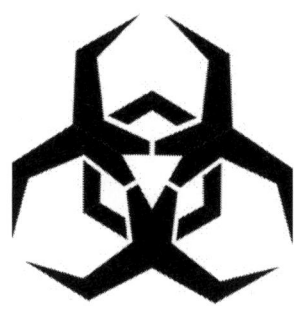

The stench of burning bodies was especially strong this morning as the soldiers on the wall burned what had piled up outside since the last large scale attack. The thick, acrid smoke hung low across the camp, creeping along the ground like fog. Mixed amongst the charred flesh smell was a hint of sweetness, which reminded Sidney of maple-cured bacon.

Gross.

After almost five months in the west Texas survivor's camp, Sidney had become accustomed to the smell. It was her daily reminder that the men and women protecting the camp were still killing the infected by the hundreds, sometimes thousands, just about every day.

The infected… They were a daily part of life now. Sometimes, when Sidney thought about the worries of her old, *modern* life, she would laugh hysterically, which didn't help with her almost pariah-like reputation in camp.

She wasn't crazy, far from it, but she was determined to survive at any cost—and to keep the life growing inside of her safe. Immediately after stumbling into the camp, pushing an orange Home Depot cart full of supplies, she'd been hit on, verbally assaulted, and one guy even tried to cop a feel of the thin, tattooed woman who, according to the slurs he shouted, was 'obviously into all the kinky shit, just look at her'. His friends rushed him to the hospital after she stabbed him in the armpit with her tiny three-inch lockback knife. He almost died before they made their way through the choked streets, but the doctors were able to save him. Apparently, there's an important artery that runs through that particular part of the human body. *Who knew?*

Since then, there'd been a few other run-ins with other refugees, none of which turned out pleasant for the other party, so she was pretty much marked as a dangerous, caged animal, and left alone. Months ago, camp officials had moved her from the tent that she'd been assigned on the requests of other residents. That was fine by her, she'd purchased a nice tent on the day the world went to hell and had never gotten to use it. Now it was her home.

Sidney left her tent by the walls—which were really just double-stacked shipping containers with mounds of dirt behind them for the tanks to drive up on—and made her way toward the latrines to use the restroom and shower. About the only thing she truly missed from her previous life were showers and bathrooms *in* her house. Well, that and alcohol, but she couldn't drink now anyways, so that wasn't too much of a concern.

"It's the crazy cat lady," a boy, no more than eight or nine, whispered to a group of children along her path.

"My mom said she's just as crazy as the infected," another said.

"I heard she steals children and cooks them in her little tent way out by the walls," Sidney replied, sending the kids scurrying in all directions.

When Sidney was alone with her cat, Rick James, she allowed herself to feel sad for what she'd become in the eyes of others. She was a genuinely nice person, who used to help people and enjoy happy hours with strangers and friends alike, but all that had changed back in the hotel in eastern Texas when she fled from Washington, DC to the Safe Zone.

She'd rented a room in a hotel the night Lincoln had turned. He'd been a raving lunatic, just like the rest of them; all semblance of his old self was gone. A gas station guard helped her and killed Lincoln, the father of the baby growing inside her now. Before his self-sacrifice to save her life—which is how he got infected—Sidney had been intent on getting an abortion. Afterward, she realized that even though they'd only known each other for six weeks or so, she loved that man and would do anything to bring their child safely into this world.

Then, the attendant at the hotel tried to rape her.

He'd been her first, and only, human kill. That hotel attendant brought the harsh realities of the new world directly into her life. Sure, she'd been in the Peace Corps and a lawyer for a non-profit battling human trafficking, so she'd seen plenty of atrocities, but the bad stuff hadn't happened to *her* until that night.

That night had helped to mold her into the person she was, the person she was becoming. And the number one rule on her expanding list was: Don't trust anyone.

Jake Murphy dragged the razor across his jawline, shaving away the stubble from the night before. He had a big day today. His platoon, 1st Platoon, Able Company, 1-36 Infantry, was the first unit that would be testing a new proof of concept to get additional food and supplies to the refugee camp.

With just over four million people in the camp, including the military, food was going quickly. Planners had brought enough supplies for half that population, not thinking the siege would last as long as it had, but the infected were relentless. Fights had been breaking out over supplies and gangs ruled entire sections of the camps, based in part on their abilities to get additional supplies.

First Lieutenant Murphy's First Platoon was going to be airlifted by six Chinook helicopters to a large Sam's Club warehouse in Midland, Texas about 290 miles away. The helicopters would land on the roof to conserve fuel and his platoon's mission was to clear the building of infected. Once that task was complete, they were to load up the five semi-trailers that recon elements had seen at the back dock with any and all foodstuffs and relevant supplies. Then the trailers were to be sling loaded under the Chinooks for the return trip to El Paso.

If they got all five trailers full, the food was only a temporary reprieve, maybe enough for two or three days, and they'd have to repeat the process at similar warehouses in Lubbock and Albuquerque, which were at the limits of the Chinook's range. After that, the lieutenant didn't know what they were supposed to do.

Situating the refugee camp at Fort Bliss in El Paso had been a brilliant tactical move by the military because of the ability to kill a lot of infected at great distances, but it was an operational nightmare to manage as supplies dwindled and they had to travel farther to find enough food for everyone. Jake didn't even want to think about the implication of putting the camp in the middle of nowhere from the strategic standpoint. It seemed just plain stupid—until he factored in the rumors about the foreign activity out west, then maybe it was smarter than he gave the planners credit for.

The people who made the decision had been trying to save as many people as possible in a short period, so he didn't have any right to second-guess their choice. He just had to live with the results and the difficulties they created.

No one had thought that the infected—a disorganized mob of insane people whose only goal in life was to attack the non-infected and spread their disease—would survive this long. Human anatomy shouldn't have been able to withstand going without food or drink that long, although truthfully, no one knew how the infected sustained themselves. They could be eating animals, insects, or even scrub brush. No one knew, and no one really cared.

He used a towel to wipe away the excess shaving cream because the camp was under a water restriction, and then slapped on some liquid aftershave. It burned like hell after the mostly dry shave, but he could handle the uncomfortable feeling.

"Alright, LT. You look as fresh as a newborn baby. Now get outta the way so us old guys can have a turn." Sergeant First Class Turner, his platoon sergeant, flashed a grizzled smile.

Jake picked up his bag and moved out of the way as the older soldier set his shaving bag on the back of the sink and began rummaging around inside it. "Alright, Sergeant. I'm going to the orderly room to get any last-minute updates from the CO. I'll meet you at the arms room at zero-seven for the additional ammo draw."

"Sounds good, sir," Sergeant Turner replied as he splashed a handful of water onto his cheeks, then proceeded to lather up his skin with shaving cream.

The lieutenant left the small company latrine and walked to the hooch that he shared with the other two single officers in the company. Grady Hallewell, the Mobile Gun System platoon leader, was married with two kids and had a house on post before everything began, so they stayed in their house — along with two additional refugee families. Jake's *hooch* wasn't much more than an area carved out in the company equipment locker area where the lieutenants had set up cots so they could always be near the office to react to situations on a moment's notice.

Not that anything exciting happened anymore. These days, the company's duties rotated between acting as roving security patrols amongst the refugees and along the wall's perimeters to ensure there weren't any breaches, and pulling kill duty at the top of the wall.

Kill duty had been exciting for the first couple of days, but now, the monotonous task was mind-numbing. At first, they killed the infected with their M-4s and then burned the bodies piled up along the wall when the mound of corpses became tall enough that they might be able to make it over the wall. Then, about a month into the siege, they'd stopped wasting so much of their ammo and switched to simply burning the infected that made it close to the wall, cutting out the middleman. It was less resource-intensive and the flyboys had a fuel farm set up somewhere out in the desert where they supposedly had access to hundreds of thousands of gallons of fuel.

The sights, sounds, and smells of burning all those *people* alive would haunt Jake for the rest of his life.

2

SURVIVOR CAMP #3, EL PASO, TEXAS
SEPTEMBER 14TH

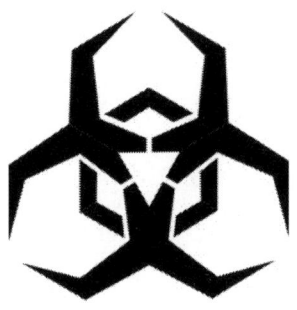

After breakfast, Sidney wandered toward the perimeter of her camp and stood, staring at the main post area with its nice housing and all the buildings. She was sick of tent city and needed to go to the big Post Exchange building where they had clothing and food, according to the camp rumor mill. Even Lincoln's pants were getting dangerously tight around her midsection.

The refugees were kept in an area heavily patrolled by armed military, under guard "for their own safety." She was sure that the leaders of the base had the same misgivings about the people in the camps that she did, but the overwhelming majority of the people were good, law-abiding citizens who were just trying to keep their families alive. The military treated everyone like they were one second away from turning into a mass-murdering asshole.

This place felt more like a prison than a safe zone.

She glanced at the sign warning all refugees to stay in the camp and not to go into the cantonment area, whatever the hell that word meant. "Dammit, I've followed the rules for months," she grumbled aloud—another habit that she'd gotten into, which contributed to her being ostracized and labeled as a crazy.

Sidney wasn't necessarily a rule-breaker, but she sure as hell didn't usually allow other people to tell her what to do. She wanted to see something else besides the endless miles of canvas tents and FEMA trailers, and today was her fucking day to do so. The rules be damned.

She stepped across the bare patch of ground where the already sparse grass was worn away by the endless foot patrols. It was an exhilarating feeling to finally take action and get out of the camp. She smiled and took three steps before the sound of a bullhorn stopped her.

"Return to the camp."

Sidney glanced around and saw one of the big, wheeled vehicles—the soldier she'd met at the first checkpoint outside the city had called it a Stryker—about two hundred feet away. They didn't have the big gun trained on her, but there was a guy with a rifle pointed in her direction.

She held up her hands to show that she didn't have any weapons.

"Put your hands down, lady. Just go back into camp."

Her hands slowly lowered and she began to turn. Then, something inside of her, the same thing that had given her the resolve to carry on after Lincoln died, made her stop. Enough was enough.

She spun back around and began walking toward the buildings in the distance.

"Hey! Stop or we'll shoot!" a frantic voice said over the speaker.

"You won't shoot me," she yelled.

The sound of heavy boots slapping on the ground startled her and she stopped. *Maybe they will shoot me.*

It only took them a few seconds to surround her. "Come on. Just go back to tent city," one of the soldiers, a female, said.

"I need some things that I can't get in *tent city*," Sidney replied tersely and tried to step around the group blocking her path.

Several of the males made comments about dragging her back or locking her up. One even suggested that they deposit her ass outside the walls since she couldn't follow the rules. The female soldier gave her companions an icy glare that silenced them before looking back at Sidney.

"What do you think you need that we haven't provided for you, ma'am?"

"Well, for starters," Sidney started to lift up the hem of her shirt, which caused two of the soldiers to level their rifles at her, making her stop her misguided attempt to show them her stomach.

"Cool it, Jenkins," the woman ordered. Sidney noticed that she had three stripes and a swooping line underneath on the patch in the middle of her tactical vest. She couldn't remember which variety of sergeant that insignia represented, but it meant that the woman was in charge of this group. "You gotta take things slow and easy, ma'am. We were just on the wall yesterday before rotating to guard duty for a week."

Sidney nodded. "Okay, yeah. Sorry. I'm pregnant." She pointed to the button fly on her jeans. The top three buttons were undone, only the bottom one was in place. "I was just going to show you that I can barely button my pants now. Pretty soon, it's gonna be impossible."

The sergeant asked, "Supply can't get you some new clothing?"

"No. They don't have *any* clothing, regardless of how much people ask," Sidney replied. "I also need prenatal vitamins, and I want to get some pillows for my back…maybe some books to pass the time."

The sergeant motioned all of her men away. "Go back to the truck. She's not going to be a problem."

The soldiers grumbled, but ultimately complied with her directive, leaving the two of them alone in the no-man's land between the refugee camp and the main base. "Okay. I think we can help with a few of those things. The PX is pretty empty, as you might imagine, but I've heard that we're going to start supply runs soon. Regardless, I'm sure there are some sweat pants or yoga pants somewhere." She took off her glove and stuck her hand out. "I'm Caitlyn."

"Sidney," she replied, taking the younger woman's hand. "Um, forgive me, I'm still new to all this. You're a sergeant?"

"Staff Sergeant," Caitlyn clarified. "It's one rank higher than a sergeant, E-5. I'm a squad leader and that's my Stryker and my squad." She gestured at the large vehicle. "How far along are you?"

"Almost six months. I can't fit into any of my old clothes."

The sergeant smiled sadly and removed her helmet, revealing blonde hair tied into a ponytail. "I had a little girl, Jocelynn. She had the brightest blue eyes and a laugh that could melt any heart, no matter how tough you were." She stopped and drew a ragged breath. Wiping the corners of her eyes with her one ungloved hand, she continued, "But that's the old world, y'know? She's in heaven now."

"I'm sorry, Caitlyn. I just..." She searched for the right words, but none came, so she settled on, "I'm *so* sorry."

The soldier nodded her head and for some reason, she didn't know why, Sidney reached out and hugged her awkwardly over the bulky tactical vest. She resisted at first, and then wrapped her arms around Sidney, pulling her tight against her body as she cried, silently at first, then in sobs of pent up sorrow. The woman's pistol dug uncomfortably into Sidney's sternum and her hands got caught in the weapon sling.

Sidney had never been one to comfort friends or be a shoulder to cry on. She'd always been the hard-nosed, no-nonsense kind of person who believed that strength and wisdom were a woman's greatest attributes. But hugging that poor girl who'd lost her child felt like the right thing to do, so she allowed herself to leave her comfort zone, to put aside her reputation as the camp psycho, and just be there for another woman in need.

After a full two minutes, maybe even three, Caitlyn disengaged and wiped away the wet lines on her cheeks. "Thank you. I haven't… It's hard being one of the only females in an all-male company, y'know? I don't have anyone who understands that sometimes, I just needed a hug." She pointed at her truck once again. "All these guys want to *fix* things, to make it better and move on. There's no bringing my daughter back. There's no fixing it."

"Are you—"

"No, no. I'm okay," Caitlyn assured her. "I'm not going to suck start my M-4 while I'm sitting on the toilet. I just needed a good, hard cry. Thank you."

Sidney nodded silently, rubbing the sergeant's upper arm as she did so. Sometimes silence was better than confusing things with words.

After another moment, Caitlyn composed herself and covered her blonde hair with the helmet she'd taken off. "We're on duty for another couple of hours. I can't let you past us unescorted, but if you come back here at noon, I can escort you to the PX to see what we can get for you over there. At the very least, some of my soldiers may have some clothes to give you."

Sidney weighed her options quickly. She could refuse and continue to try and break the rules—and lose the one potential ally she'd just gained—or she could go back to the camp, wait a few hours and come back here to be escorted, legally, onto the main post. It was a no-brainer.

"Thank you, Caitlyn. Thank you so much! I'll see you in a couple of hours. Okay?"

3

MIDLAND-ODESSA, TEXAS
SEPTEMBER 14TH

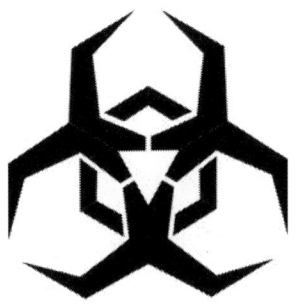

Lieutenant Murphy sat back against the canvas webbing that ran along the fuselage as the giant rotor blades above him thrummed steadily. They'd been in the air over the west Texas desert for an hour and a half before they sat down at a forward area refueling point. It was what the rotorheads called a "FARP," because the Chinook only had a range of 400 miles without extra fuel bladders mounted inside—something that Command decided was too heavy for the birds if they were going to get every scrap of food and supplies from that Sam's Club in one go.

Jake's platoon had pulled additional safety at the site where helicopters from Bliss had previously dropped full fuel bladders. With the fuel from the FARP, they'd be able to make it all the way to the warehouse and back to El Paso without stopping again. Thankfully, the refueling operation was uneventful and everyone had loaded back into the choppers for the last leg to Midland.

"Look at that!" someone shouted from somewhere near the door gunners.

Jake looked toward the front of the helicopter and saw one of his soldiers, he couldn't tell which one, pointing out the open hatch where the port-side door gunner had his hand over his mouth, holding the microphone close to his lips. He nodded and pulled back the charging handle on the M-240 mounted on a rail in the hatch, then slammed it forward, hunching down slightly so his eyes lined up with the iron sights. He depressed the butterfly triggers and the machine gun began to rock and roll.

Jake unbuckled his lap harness and turned in the flimsy seat so he could see out of the Plexiglas bubble set into the Chinook's fuselage. The bird wasn't trying to evade any enemy rockets or fly in any fancy maneuvers, so he was fine just holding on to a cable that ran the length of the helicopter for support.

The downtown area of Midland bristled with several high-rise buildings, densely packed into a few blocks. The rest of the city spread out for what seemed like miles in the hazy morning sun. Down on the ground, thousands of infected ran through the streets of Midland toward the sounds of the helicopters approaching the city from the southwest.

Soon, the gunner on the starboard side began to fire, followed quickly by the ramp gunner at the back of the helicopter. From his angle at the window, he saw hundreds of shell casings falling from the helicopter adjacent to them, the brass twinkling in the sunlight as it fell.

It was beautiful.

Other than the gunners raining down death from above, there was nothing else to see that they hadn't seen a hundred times before. The fucking infected ran toward the sight and sound of the helicopters, heedless of obstacles, barriers, and even each other. It was as if their brains could only process the fact that there was potential prey in the area and nothing else mattered.

Just what the hell are they infected with? Jake wondered for the thousandth time. *And even if we knew, is there a cure besides killing them?*

His men often accused him of keeping secrets from them, since he was an officer. In truth, he knew just as much as the rest of the grunts on the ground — or, in the air in this case. The captain didn't know anything more, and as far as either of them knew, neither did Spartan Six, the commander of 1-36 Infantry — Jake's battalion.

If anyone knew anything about the nature of the disease, it sure as hell wasn't the men and women on the ground fighting the creatures on a daily basis.

Someone patted his knee hard enough to make him think it was intentional and not just an accident in the cramped space. He turned back around and Specialist Barrera, his driver and radio telephone operator, or RTO for short, yelled something, pointing toward the front of the bird. Jake shook his head, pointing to his own ear in turn, and eased himself down off the seat.

"What?" he shouted into Barrera's ear to be heard over the Chinook's engines, the gunfire, and the earplugs that they all wore.

"Pilots want to talk to you," the soldier replied.

Jake gave him a thumbs up and made his way toward the cockpit, slipping between the knees of soldiers stretched out into the center of the helicopter and the crates of extra ammunition secured there. They expected a fight.

When he finally made it to the cockpit, one of the pilots, a Chief Warrant Officer 3, lifted his darkened visor and handed him a pair of over-the-ear headphones with an attached microphone. Jake accepted them and took off his helmet so he could put them on. Once the cups were over his ears, the heavy staccato of the machine guns just a few feet away deadened to dull thuds.

"Can you hear me, LT?" the pilot who'd given him the headset asked.

Jake fumbled with the transmit button for a moment and then replied, "Yeah. What's up, Chief?"

"You're the ground unit commander, sir. We need to know if you still want to proceed with the mission."

He looked out the cockpit's windows, which afforded him a complete 180-degree view. The cities of Midland and Odessa were officially about two miles apart, but over time, they'd grown together. Their pre-infection population had been about 250,000 people combined; there was no telling how many of those remained.

It sure as hell looked like every one of them from up here.

Jake considered his options. Captain Massey's orders were to not take any unnecessary risks, but he knew the food situation would soon turn desperate back at Bliss, so sooner rather than later, they'd be forced to try these types of missions anyway. He had two full platoons of infantrymen, battle-hardened and proven in the current conflict, at his command. Plus, they'd burned a ton of fuel to bring the six helicopters all this way.

"I want to draw them away from the warehouse," Jake finally answered after what seemed like an eternity. "Swing out over the north part of town and then circle back to the target building. Think we can do that?"

"Sure, but we only have enough fuel to fuck around for about thirty minutes, sir."

Jake nodded and keyed the microphone again. "Okay. What can my guys do to help?"

"Other than resupplying the gunners with ammo, just sit back and enjoy the ride," the warrant officer replied. "We'll tell the other birds what we're going to do, then move out."

Jake took off the headset and hung it on a hook beside the small cockpit opening, then shuffled back to his seat, tapping the soldiers on the helmet as he went by. "Keep the guns supplied with ammo!" he shouted, gesturing between the cans of ammunition and the door gunners. "We're gonna circle around the city and then land."

He told every third soldier the same thing, relying on the fact that they'd pass the word to the guys who didn't get the message firsthand. Once he was sure everyone had an idea of what was going to happen, he sat back down in his seat and looked out the window. The helicopter on the far flank had lowered by several hundred feet, their guns firing point-blank into thousands of infected, literally mowing them down with well-placed and accurate gunfire from the M-240s.

Jake knew that the infected weren't like some mythical zombie. They didn't need nearly impossible headshots to kill them. They could bleed out and die from severed arteries, fire would kill them, and they could be shocked and die. Anything that would kill a regular human would kill the infected as well — except little things like pain or broken bones didn't bother them, which is why some of the soldiers insisted on calling the creatures zombies.

The helicopters, which to Jake looked like they'd spread out significantly, continued to spit lead to the sides and rear as the formation circled northward, the infected following away from the target building—and dying—by the hundreds.

They made a giant loop, all the way to the far side of the city and hovered low, sending giant, billowing clouds of dust skyward. The infected continued to chase after them and Jake worried that they may actually be drawing *more* of them from the surrounding countryside. But, it was the best option they had.

After hovering low for around five minutes, the formation of helicopters turned and headed slowly into the dessert, leading the mob further out into the desert as the tail gunners blasted them. Several more minutes of this technique passed, and then the helicopters picked up speed, moving far ahead of their pursuers before gaining elevation and banking back around to the southwest.

Midland shrank in the distance below them and then the formation once again turned back toward the city, approaching from the south. The pilots flashed the red interior lights, indicating that they were on approach. To Jake, who'd never participated in a real-world helicopter operation outside of Ranger School, it seemed that they were impossibly far away and much too high to be on approach for landing. He wasn't a pilot, though, he was just a passenger for this leg of the trip and he knew that, so he sat back and buckled in.

His stomach flipped and felt like it would burst from his throat as the helicopters dropped rapidly from the sky. The only thing he could see through the open cargo ramp at the back of the bird was blue sky, so he had to hope that they were headed to the target building as planned and not some emergency mission abort from Higher that he didn't know anything about.

Jake's view changed from blue to a muddy mixture of sky and earth on the far horizon, and then the wheels touched down on the roof of the building. He unbuckled his harness and followed the man in front of him, running hunched over along a gray rooftop toward the lip of the building. Behind him, he heard the big engines on several Chinook helicopters shutting down in the hopes that they fooled the infected.

He pulled up and took in his surroundings. All six of the helicopters had landed on the roof of the Sam's Club warehouse, spaced more or less evenly across the surface in between the air conditioning units. The first thing he noticed about his surroundings was the incredibly horrible smell. The entire building smelled like spoiled meat. It made his stomach turn and he pulled his t-shirt up over his nose.

Around him, soldiers scrambled in every direction toward the building's perimeter. His platoon and 2nd Platoon, led by Second Lieutenant Brian Mirman, gave him eighty-four light infantrymen to do the dirty work inside, plus he had seven sniper/spotter teams from battalion. The snipers would begin picking off any stragglers in the area with their silenced rifles while the grunts cleared the building and began loading the semi-trailers at the dock.

Jake saw Sergeant First Class Turner in an open space, furiously gesturing toward points along the building's perimeter and beginning the process of securing the facility. He smiled, knowing that the tough old veteran was screaming at the squad leaders to get everyone into position—he was just doing it quietly.

He glanced behind at the edge of the building where a sniper team was already engaging targets. From where he crouched, the muffled sounds of their rifles were barely audible, lost to the sound of the wind.

4

SURVIVOR CAMP #3, EL PASO, TEXAS
SEPTEMBER 14TH

"No, I'm—" She stopped and composed her thoughts. "Private Lopez," she read the man's nametape aloud. "There's a soldier that I met earlier, a woman named Caitlyn. Blonde hair? She was supposed to meet me here at noon to help me get some clothes that fit."

"I'm sorry, ma'am. I don't know anybody named Caitlyn," the soldier blocking her way grunted.

"Dammit. She's a staff sergeant...had a little girl who died. I don't know her last name."

"Wait, a female staff sergeant?" The soldier turned to his partner. "Does she mean Sergeant Wyatt? From third platoon?"

The other kid shrugged. "I don't know, man." He scratched his arm vigorously. "I don't know what her first name is."

Lopez shifted uneasily and Sidney immediately and took an involuntary step backward. "Why you scratchin' so much, Thomas?"

Thomas stopped, mid-scratch and lifted both hands. "Take it easy, Lopez. I'm just itchy from the shitty laundry detergent."

"Let me see your arm."

"Hey, man. I—"

"*Now*, Thomas!" Lopez said, raising his rifle.

Sidney stumbled backward, tripping on the gravel path surrounding the camp, and fell, hard onto her butt. The impact jarred her stomach and she clutched her abdomen in pain.

Lopez risked a quick glance at her, giving Thomas an opening. "Look out!" she cried.

Thomas slapped the barrel of the rifle away causing Lopez to fire a round into the gravel near Sidney's feet and sending jagged shards of rock in all directions. She scrambled backward in an attempt to separate herself from these two.

Thomas had stepped inside the reach of Lopez and punched upward into the other soldier's chin. Lopez crumpled like a rock as the roar of engines flaring to life and tires crunching on gravel echoed across the afternoon. Two Stryker vehicles arrived at the sight of the altercation within seconds.

"Is she infected?" someone yelled through the vehicle's speaker system. *"Did she bite Lopez?"*

Sidney looked around, wondering who they were talking about before realizing that they meant her. She threw up her hands, wincing as the gravel tore into her tailbone. Too late, she felt blood begin to run down her arm from a wound in her wrist. She'd been hit by a piece of rock when Lopez fired his gun.

"Wait!" she screamed. "That's from a piece of rock when he shot his gun."

"Don't move!" a voice right behind her shouted, making her jump.

"Please! I didn't do anything. It was that Thompson kid—I mean Thomas. Private Thomas."

Rough hands grabbed her and pain exploded in her wrist as the soldier pressed against the injury. The barrel of a weapon pressed roughly against her temple as another soldier ensured she didn't try anything foolish. Her hands were wrenched behind her and she could feel herself being flipped over. "Please! I'm pregnant!" she pleaded.

The soldier didn't listen, instead, he continued to lift her wrists toward the middle of her back and press her shoulders down. In a moment, pure momentum would fling her onto her stomach.

"Stop it!" a strong female voice bellowed. "What the fuck are you doing to that refugee?"

Sidney looked up and saw her new friend storming up from the Fort Bliss side of the Safe Zone. "Caitlyn! Caitlyn, help me," she pleaded. "They're going to push me onto the baby."

"Sidney?" she asked in surprise. "Let her go right now, Specialist."

"She might be infected, Sergeant," the man holding her wrists replied. "She attacked Lopez."

Sidney glanced over to where the private was being lifted into a sitting position by a few of the other soldiers. "No. The other guy was scratching and Lopez asked him about it," she said quickly. "He attacked Lopez and he shot his rifle. Some of the rocks hit me in the wrist, that's why I'm bleeding."

Caitlyn looked between Sidney and Lopez before saying, "Let her go."

Sidney's hands were released and the soldier holding the rifle pulled it away from her face, but kept it pointed at her from about twelve inches away. Caitlyn crouched in front of Sidney while she touched her injured wrist lightly. "Who was the soldier, Sidney? Did you happen to get—"

"Thomas," Sidney answered immediately. "Private Thomas."

"Where's Thomas?" Caitlyn asked, standing quickly.

"He was just—" The specialist who'd waylaid her looked around. "I don't know," he admitted.

"Find him, you idiot." Caitlyn's boots tromped across the gravel. "Sergeant Kline. Where's— There you are. Where's Thomas? This refugee said he was scratching and then attacked Lopez."

"He, uh—"

"Call it up. *Now*," Caitlyn ordered.

"Yes, Sergeant," the other noncommissioned officer replied and disappeared behind the Stryker.

The base alarms began to peal almost immediately.

"ALERT! ALERT! THERE HAS BEEN A POSSIBLE INFECTION INSIDE THE WALLS. ALL PERSONNEL ARE TO REPORT TO THEIR DUTY STATIONS IMMEDIATELY. REFUGEES ARE ORDERED TO YOUR MUSTER LOCATIONS. I REPEAT—"

The message repeated itself and Sidney was already tuning it out.

"Come on, Sidney," Caitlyn said as she helped her to her feet. "You've got to report to your muster location and I've got to go find my squad."

Sidney nodded in disbelief. How had one of the soldiers gotten infected? It was her worst fear, something that had almost caused her to leave *before* she became trapped behind the walls of Fort Bliss. "What do I do if it starts to spread?" she mumbled.

"It won't. We'll get him," Caitlyn assured her.

"He was just right here," Sidney stated. "It's only been a minute or two."

"If he really is infected, then—"

Several shots rang out from nearby in rapid succession, interrupting her. Five seconds later, one final report told the story as plainly as if someone had told her exactly what was happening.

"We got him!" one of the soldiers shouted. "We got him."

"Hold on," Caitlyn said, stepping away from Sidney, who probed the wound on her wrist gingerly, trying to ascertain if anything was broken or if there was any rock stuck inside.

Everything seemed fine, so she examined the cut. It wasn't bad enough that she'd need stiches, but it hurt like a sonofabitch. Everything had happened so fast. So incredibly fast. From the time Lopez asked him about his itching to the time she was surrounded by Strykers was less than two minutes. They were lucky the trucks were so close.

That's all it was: pure, dumb luck. If Thomas hadn't been noticed for a few hours and then turned… Sidney shuddered, remembering the stories she'd overheard refugees from the FEMA camps tell as she sat in her little tent between the larger army tents. The infected had swept through those places quickly, tens of thousands of people died in those *Safe Zone* camps.

"Okay, let's get you cleaned up, huh?" Caitlyn said, interrupting her thoughts.

"Oh, it's okay."

"No, it's not," her new friend replied, gripping Sidney's hand lightly and lifting it up to examine the wound on her wrist. "They won't let you in the PX for one thing. For the other, I don't want to have to explain to everyone we see about what happened. We'll just put a small bandage on your hand and clean up the blood."

"*ATTENTION ON THE BASE,*" the Giant Voice system blared from speakers mounted on telephone poles throughout the base. "*THE THREAT HAS

BEEN NEUTRALIZED. RETURN TO YOUR NORMAL ACTIVITIES."

"Neutralized," Sidney grunted. "Is that Army-speak for 'killed'?"

Caitlyn squeezed Sidney's hand gently. "Don't you worry your pretty little head about it. They took care of the threat."

Sidney shook her head. "Thomas said he was having an allergic reaction to the cheap laundry detergent. What if he just freaked out at being accused of being an infected?"

"Then he was stupid."

"He was just a kid," Sidney countered. "We all do dumb shit when we get scared. Hell, I was just begging like a leper in Karachi when I thought they were gonna hurt my baby."

"That's understandable, Sidney. There's nothing to be ashamed of."

She waved off the effort to comfort her. "That kid was just shot and killed with no evidence that anything was wrong with him."

"If he wasn't infected, then he shouldn't have run off," Caitlyn replied. "I'm sorry that it's a shock to you, Sidney, but that's just the way things are now."

She nodded glumly, wondering if she'd inadvertently been the cause of Thomas' death since she'd told everyone what happened, sending them off to hunt the kid. It was another example of how serious everyday life was in this place. Nothing could be taken for granted.

Then again, he *could* have been infected and she'd saved the camp. She'd never know.

"Okay, now that it's over, we had an appointment to try to get you some new clothes."

"Yeah, um… Okay," she replied, glancing away.

Caitlyn stepped in front of her. "I've asked around about you, Sidney. Talked to a bunch of soldiers and some people in the camp. They—"

Sidney's eyes snapped up to look the soldier in the face. "You did? Why?"

"I just like to know who I'm dealing with. Old habits die hard. People here say that you're a hard-nosed bitch. That true?"

It was Sidney's turn to shrug as she repeated, "Old habits die hard."

"I like it," Caitlyn said with a broad smile that showed her whitened teeth. "Come on. I don't have a vehicle, so we'll have to walk, but it's only about two miles from here."

As Sidney stepped off to catch up to her new friend, she purposefully forced the thoughts from her head that she may have been responsible for an innocent man's death. Caitlyn was right; the stupid kid shouldn't have run.

That, and I'm a hard-nosed bitch.

5

MIDLAND-ODESSA, TEXAS
SEPTEMBER 14TH

"Alright, how do we get inside?" Jake asked his platoon sergeant.

"Shit, sir," Sergeant First Class Turner said after he spat a glob of chewing tobacco saliva onto the Sam's Club roof. "What we thought were doors into the warehouse from the satellite photo just led to a large HVAC unit."

Jake looked around at the men on the roof standing beside the helicopters. They'd come all this way, thinking that getting inside the building would be the easy part. They hadn't expected any real risks until *after* they'd filled the trailers and had to go outside to ground level to sling load them. "Do we have enough rope to rappel into the building through the skylights?"

The old NCO thought about it for a moment before answering. "Yes, sir. We should have plenty, but to be honest, I'm not sure how many of the guys know what the fuck they're doing. Somebody'll probably fall and get fucked up."

"Hmmm…" Jake mumbled, thinking through the problem. "Wait. This is fucking *Sam's Club*. They sell those big-ass ladders in there. We just have to have one or two soldiers rappel inside and then bring over a few ladders."

Turner slapped him hard on the back of his tactical vest. "Whoo wee! See, that's why you get paid the big bucks, sir."

Jake chuckled. "I haven't been paid in more than five months, Sergeant." He affected a hurt look and continued, "Are you telling me the Army's holding out on me?"

"Nah, sir. Just sayin'. How many men do you want me to send down?"

"Let's break out one of the skylights first, see if there are any infected down in there, and then once the coast is clear, like, four guys?"

"Sounds good, sir."

The NCO stood up and started giving hand and arm signals to bring the squad leaders to him. As he did so, Brian Mirman, the 2nd Platoon's platoon leader, stepped over to him. "Hey, Jake. What's the plan?"

He outlined what he planned and Brian smiled. "You know, I'm a climber."

"Really?"

"Yeah, man. I did all fifty-eight of the 14ers while I was in college—well, I did three of them in high school, but I still count it."

Jake looked at him dumbly. "I have no idea what you're talking about, Brian."

"The 14ers?"

"Yeah."

"Oh! I guess if you're not from Colorado or—"

"Just spill it, man."

"There are fifty-eight mountain peaks over 14,000 feet in the state of Colorado. Collectively, they're called the 14ers and I've climbed 'em all."

"Does that mean you're good at rock climbing or something?"

"Yeah," Brian replied. "And, rappelling. I'm a certified rappel master—I'm the guy you need on this mission, bro!"

"Okay. So there's one. I need three more volunteers."

"I know one guy, Corporal Gaspar from my platoon. He's been to the Army Mountain Warfare Course out in Vermont. He'll probably be all over it."

"Okay. Go talk to him and come back here when you're done."

Within ten minutes, Jake had his insertion team standing by. Brian and Corporal Gaspar had helped the other two with tying Swiss seat harnesses from a single piece of rope. It was pretty standard stuff for people who'd gone through the Army Air Assault course or Ranger School, but neither of the other two volunteers had done so; they were just willing to try to go through the hole and potentially be dangling from a rope over the grasping hands of hundreds of infected.

Or, the building could be completely abandoned, they didn't know yet.

"Alright, sir. I'm breaking the skylight," Sergeant Turner said.

"Go for it."

The platoon sergeant slammed a large wrench into the plastic skylight. If there wasn't the potential for some of his men to get hurt, Jake would have laughed at the comically oversized tool that Sergeant

Turner had gotten from one of the Chinook crew chiefs.

The clear plastic resisted against the first hit. After the third, a thin crack appeared. "Fuck this. Stand back, fellas," Sergeant Turner said, sliding his rifle around to the front.

He stood and fired four rounds, stitching a line of holes in the material.

"Goddammit, Sergeant!" Jake hissed. "We're trying to be quiet."

"Those fucking helicopters made enough noise to wake the dead, sir. I—"

"Poor choice of words, man," Lieutenant Mirman mumbled.

"Fuck it, sir," Turner said, slamming the wrench against the plastic. It broke through and stuck. He wiggled it back and forth a few times, pulling hard until it came free. Another two well-placed hits and most of the plastic fell away.

"There you go, gentlemen," Turner said, holding his arms wide. "Ask and ye shall receive."

Jake looked through the opening. "Seems clear," he said.

"Hold on, sir." Sergeant Turner pointed to the nearest helicopter. "Specialist, go get a flare from the crew chief."

The nearest soldier jogged off and returned with a flare moments later. Sergeant Turner lit it and dropped it through the opening. He peered inside for several minutes, waiting for something to be drawn toward the red light. Nothing came and he gave the group waiting around the hole a thumbs up.

"Alright, I'll take the lead," Lieutenant Mirman said enthusiastically, wrapping the rope around the carabiner.

"Go for it, buddy. Check your six," Jake said.

Mirman smiled and pulled on the rope, ensuring it was secured to a tie down anchor set into the floor of the nearest bird. "Here goes nothing."

He leaned out over the hole, his upper body and legs formed an "L" before he pushed off and disappeared from sight. Jake looked over the edge, his friend was about halfway to the ground already. It wasn't long before he was on the ground and looking up.

"I'm down," Mirman called, pulling the rope through the carabiner quickly.

"How's it look?"

"Good. There doesn't seem to be anything down here." Mirman turned around quickly with his rifle up. "I think we're cl—"

"Oh my God!" a woman's voice drifted up from below. "Oh thank, God! We're saved."

6

NEAR TYRONE, OKLAHOMA
SEPTEMBER 14TH

"Aww yeah! That's the one we wanted, buddy!"

Tim glanced at his partner in crime as he pressed the button that led to his winch on the front bumper. The cable went up and over a large tree limb. The winch would pull their target off the ground up out of the way of the other loonies. He and Russ had secured a large rope noose on the other end of the cable and they'd caught their prey with their superior "fishing" skills.

A thin, mostly-nude woman thrashed wildly against the rope cinched tightly around her waist. Her body was covered in dozens of scrapes, cuts, and bruises, as well as months of piss and shit. She probably smelled awful. But underneath all that filth was their prize: A woman—and a pretty fine looking one to boot.

Now all they had to do was defend her.

"Alright, she's up," Tim grunted, pointing at the woman dangling above the crowd of crazies. "Time to earn her now."

He stepped out of the truck and grabbed his homemade mace. When the infected trapped in the pit below saw him, they began to snarl wildly and started to scream, as they had when Russ honked the horn to lead them to the trap. They'd been fairly docile up until that point; the large hole they found themselves in was as good as any other place they'd wandered over the past several months. But now that an uninfected human was within their grasp, they began to tear at themselves and each other in an effort to reach him.

"Oh, calm down. Your turn's coming," Tim said, tugging off one of his Kevlar gloves and tucking it under his arm. Then he unzipped his pants and began to piss onto the pathetic creatures below. He angled his dick, laughing as he sprayed urine into the open mouth of an upturned face. It began to choke. "Hey. Hey, Russ. Look at that one. I filled its mouth with piss."

His brother got a good laugh, and even took out his cell phone to snap a picture. "Oh man. I wish the Internet was still working. This sonofabitch would go viral."

Tim grinned along, but found the other man's longing for the Internet to be annoying. To be honest, he was happy that the old world was gone. All the drama and bullshit was in the past and every day he had to test himself to stay alive. *This* was living.

"Alright, the fun's over," Tim said, tucking his junk away and then scratching at his scraggly red beard. He didn't know what his heritage was, but the red beard was sure a surprise when it grew out. *Irish or some other shit*, he'd thought.

"No way, buddy," Russ said. "This *is* part of the fun." Even through the face shield, Tim could see the excited gleam in his eye.

He pulled his remaining glove back onto his hand, clenching his fist and relishing the feel of the hard plastic knuckles integrated into it. Tim enjoyed the close-up work too, it didn't matter that it was inherently more dangerous. But he was also smart. Trying to take on more than one or two loonies at a time and a guy could get fucked up quickly. It was best to use a standoff weapon in that case.

His weapon of choice was a five-foot length of rebar sharpened to a point on one end. On the other end, he'd welded a solid ball of metal that could be used as a long club if there was enough room to swing it. He hadn't gotten to use it like that in combat yet, but he was sure the day would come. Russ just used a damn metal closet rod that he'd welded a bowie knife to. Tim loved his brother, but he had no imagination.

Tim poked idly toward the eye of a male infected, trying to see how much pressure it took to pop its eyeball, but the damn thing grabbed the rebar, trying to pull him down into the pit. *"Ungh!"* Tim grunted as he pushed hard to break the loony's grasp. The rebar slid through the man's hands and found a home through the eye socket into the brain. He dropped like a rock, reminding Tim that he needed to keep his wits about him and not let his guard down.

They spent the next five minutes poking and stabbing at the infected until the twenty or so they'd lured to the pit were dead. The two men grinned at each other and shook gloved hands. "Nice work, brother."

"Same to you, Russ." Tim looked up at the thrashing woman. "Got the chloroform ready?"

"Hold on. I gotta go get it from the Jeep."

"Get my catching pole too, man. I'm gonna check to make sure the electric fence is holding."

"Sure thing, hoss."

While Russ went about the preparations for getting their prize home in one piece, Tim walked the perimeter of their capture cage. Outside, several infected lay on the ground, unmoving, while a woman held onto the fence, smoke pouring from her hairline as she cooked from the inside out.

"Stupid mother fucker," Tim groaned. "You're gonna short out the fence."

He bent over and picked up several rocks, then walked to within three feet of the dead woman. After the fourth rock, hurled with all the might that a former high school pitcher could muster, he knocked the woman's fingers away. She fell backward, separating the skin-to-fence contact and avoiding a potential short circuit of the system.

There weren't any more of them milling around, so he returned to the pit, where Russ stood pouring a dark liquid onto a rag. "Soak it good this time," Tim directed, picking up the dog catcher's pole that he'd owned for years to help with livestock around the farm.

He started to maneuver the loop over the woman's head and then remembered that he needed the winch controls. "Dammit," he muttered, placing the pole on the ground. He went to the Jeep and grabbed the small control box, careful to feed it back through the window without damaging it.

Once he was ready to go again, he hooked the loop in place on her neck, then carefully choreographed pulling her toward the edge of the pit as he lowered the winch. "Watch out for her hands," he warned.

"I know, dammit." Russ grunted, working his way inside her grasp to place the rag against her mouth and nose. "Whew! This one smells awful."

"It's been six or seven months since this all started," Tim replied, straining to keep her as still as possible. "We'll get her cleaned up."

The struggling stopped as Russ held the rag over her face and her body went limp. They knew from experience that the chloroform only lasted about ten to fifteen minutes on the infected before they were awake again, so they didn't have a lot of time to work.

They tossed her unceremoniously to the ground and handcuffed her arms above her head to the grill of the Jeep. Russ jammed a hard piece of rubber into her mouth and Tim straddled her. It only took him eight minutes to pull out her rotting teeth with a pair of pliers as Tim assisted, moving the rubber around as needed.

Next, they slapped duct tape over her mouth and taped a pair of gloves onto her hands in case she woke up while they transported her. They weren't entirely sure what part of the infected transferred the disease, but before the news went off the air permanently, they knew that scratches could transmit the deadly virus—although Tim suspected that it was when infected fluids got into those scratches, not the breaking of the skin itself.

"Alright, dose her again and let's get out of here," Tim directed.

Russ complied and then they removed one handcuff, dragging her to the back of the Jeep where Tim had a wire mesh rack attached to the trailer hitch. It was supposed to be for extra gas cans or coolers, but the men found that it worked nicely for securing an infected outside of the vehicle. They strapped her down using a variety of ratchet straps, bungee cords and the handcuffs themselves.

When they were satisfied that their prize wouldn't bounce off, Tim started up the Jeep while Russ ran to the solar powered generator. He turned off the fence and then opened the gate for Tim. After the Jeep passed, he closed the gate and hopped inside.

Tim extended his fist to Russ with a wide grin. The younger man bumped it with his own. "Let's go get this bitch cleaned up."

"Dibs on first go round," Russ yelled, slapping the dashboard.

"Whatever, dude. Just make sure you wear two or three condoms. Don't want another scare like we had with the last one."

7

SURVIVOR CAMP #3, EL PASO, TEXAS
SEPTEMBER 15TH

"Tell me the truth. Does my ass look big in these?" Sidney asked.

Rick James *meowed* in response from his perch on top of the two backpacks that she kept packed and ready to go at a moment's notice.

"Ah, what do you know?" she said, waving her hand dismissively. She sat heavily onto her air mattress and looked at the haul that Caitlyn had helped her secure. She'd gotten two pairs of sweatpants, a legitimate pair of pregnancy jeans, three large tank tops, and even a pair of extra-large basketball shorts. None of it was fashionable, but by God, it was exactly what she needed.

As a bonus, she'd been able to get a four-pack of newborn onesies and three more 12-month old outfits. Plus, there was an infant car seat over in the corner by the bags. She'd questioned the seat initially, but Caitlyn had told her that it was a lifesaver instead of always carrying the baby. The seat was one of those that was supposed to fit onto a stroller, so she could always just snap it onto her shopping cart for long trips around the refugee camp.

Caitlyn had seemed genuinely happy to help her pick out all of the baby gear, and added pacifiers, diapers, and wipes to her list. The employees had long since abandoned their jobs, so the MPs watching the store had let her walk out with everything once the Staff Sergeant showed her ID card. No questions asked.

Last night had been the first truly restful night that Sidney had had in a long time. The new, better-fitting clothing, along with the baby essentials, made her feel like there really was some type of hope. Hope for herself and the baby, of course, but hope for humanity as well. The soldier hadn't needed to take time out of her day to help, but she'd chosen to do so.

Sidney leaned back on her mattress and allowed herself a moment to forget about everything. The infected...the survivors...the lack of food... She allowed herself to think about Caitlyn, with her cute little upturned nose, those full lips. The soldier's unprecedented kindness was incredibly sexy. Her hand started to inch downward as she wondered what her new friend would look like naked; better yet, what would the two of them look like naked together?

She wasn't a lesbian—hell, she was pregnant with her former lover's baby—but she'd been with women many times over the years, often preferring how soft and accommodating even the most forceful women could be behind closed doors. Her lips curved upward in pleasure as the images of Caitlyn that she'd conjured up responded to her direction.

It was over far sooner than it should have been and she lay, staring up at the seams of her tent above. She felt entirely relaxed—again, something that hadn't happened since arriving at the refugee camp. She felt like she could take on the world. She felt like...

She felt like she could sleep.

Her alarm clock buzzed loudly and incessantly. She reached to her left and slapped at where the damn thing should have been, but it wasn't and it kept wailing at her.

Wailing? That wasn't right.

Sidney's exhausted mind stirred slowly, unwilling to leave the blissful dream realm behind. As she emerged from sleep, she was assaulted by noise and light from the midday sun, shining directly down on her tent.

"*...NOT A DRILL,*" the camp's Big Voice system echoed. "*RESIDENTS OF REFUGEE CAMP NUMBER THREE ARE ORDERED TO CEASE ACTIVITIES AND RETURN TO YOUR BARRACKS IMMEDIATELY. IF YOU DO NOT COMPLY, YOU RISK BEING FIRED UPON.*"

"What the hell?" she asked aloud.

Rick James hissed from behind the backpacks and the first noises from outside began to filter in between the announcements. People were shouting and feet scattered gravel in all directions nearby.

The alarms and instructions to cease continued to blare through the speakers as Sidney cautiously unzipped the top of her tent's entry flap. Through the mesh, she could see people running toward the mess tents. For a moment, she panicked, remembering how the infected ran toward sounds, and she wondered if the soldier from the day before *had* been infected and spread the disease before getting shot.

Then, she relaxed slightly, realizing that no one that she saw was bleeding or screaming incoherently. Instead, there was a full-on riot occurring. It was a mile away, but her tent was on a rise near the wall so she could see that people were mobbing the trucks that brought food to the camp. They streamed from all over, thousands of them, headed toward the soldiers. The idiots were rioting over food shortages.

She grabbed the small pair of binoculars she'd picked up at REI and adjusted them as she watched what was happening. Almost immediately, she saw that it was going to get bad and grimaced as several arms at the back of the crowd reared back, holding bricks and rocks. They threw their makeshift projectiles at the soldiers. Most fell ineffectively into the crowd itself, or pelted harmlessly off the sides of the truck. One soldier, however, was hit and he slumped forward over the side of the truck. The hungry mob grabbed his clothing and pulled him down into the crowd.

Then, the worst thing imaginable that could have happened did. Someone—or several someones, she couldn't tell—fired guns at the soldiers. The refugees had been allowed to keep their weapons as a means of defense against the infected, but no one had foreseen this extended period of detention. Several of the soldiers in the trucks, likely other refugees who'd joined the Civilian Division upon entering the camp, crumpled from the gunfire.

After that, everything was a blur of sights and sounds. The Army returned fire, blasting the crowd at point-blank range with machine guns. Sidney watched for a moment in horror until a round tore through the tent's fabric, only a few feet from her.

"Shit!" she yelped, jumping back from the front of the tent. She looked around her small space for any type of cover. All she came up with was the backpacks. Rick James hissed at her as she moved the packs so they covered her upper body; her legs were exposed, but there was nothing to be done about that.

The firing continued, even intensified as more of the refugees joined the fight with actual weapons instead of just rocks and sticks. It went on for what seemed like forever, neither side gaining the upper hand, while women and children were caught in the crossfire.

Her tent rattled and then the zipper jerked violently downward. Sidney recoiled in terror as the sneering face of a man appeared in the opening. It took her a moment to recognize that it was a man she hadn't seen since her first day at the camp, since the incident.

It was him. It was the man who'd tried to molest her. The one that she'd stabbed. His face was much thinner and more tan, but there was no mistaking him. It was the same guy.

"You home, bitch?" he asked, wildly working the zipper. It stuck on the fabric, like it sometimes did when she tried to unzip it too fast. He cursed and yanked on the small metal tab, trying to break it free. "I'm gonna make you pay, cunt."

The zipper stoppage gave Sidney time to fumble in the backpack for the large kitchen knife hidden there. It was the same one that she'd used to defend herself against the hotel clerk in eastern Texas. She bore the scar across her chest to match the width of the blade as well.

The zipper tore free from the fabric and it slid the rest of the way without protest. The man stepped through, glancing left and right, and then back at her. "Nice place. I see you've been hoarding shit."

"I'm not hoarding any—"

"Save it, bitch," he said, cutting her off. "We saw you with that soldier bitch, bringing bags of food and boxes of stuff back here to your tent."

"Baby clothes!" she screeched, standing and holding the knife unsteadily in front of her with both hands.

"What the fuck do you think you're going to do with that?"

"Whatever I have to," she replied coolly, feeling oddly calm. The knife stopped wavering.

"All this is your fault," the man said, jerking his head toward the riot outside. "Now that we know they're keeping stuff from us, we want more."

His words startled her. The riot was because they'd seen her with a car seat and diapers? Was everyone insane? "It's some goddamned baby clothes and sweat pants, you fucking psychopath."

He used her confusion to his advantage and lunged across the small tent, grabbing her by the wrist. She punched at him with her left hand, but he easily blocked the blows with his forearm. He squeezed her wrist and the knife fell away.

"You've got some spunk in you," he said, leering at her. "When I'm done, you'll have a lot of *my* spunk in you." He laughed, obviously thinking his joke was clever.

"You won't get away with rape, asshole. They'll fry your ass."

Ignoring her, he continued. "Then, I'll cut that precious baby from your stomach and roast it like a chicken over the campfire. So juicy. You ever wonder…"

He continued to talk, but his words were drowned out by the swarm of bees buzzing in her head. The idea that he'd dare to threaten her baby enraged her beyond the capacity to think. Her vision turned red, there was no way that she'd let anyone harm her child. *Ever.*

She rammed her head forward, hitting the man in the bridge of his nose, shattering the cartilage and unleashing a torrent of blood. He released her wrist to grab at his ruined nose and she pounced forward, clawing at his eyes. Her body felt the edge of her fingertip sink into the man's soft eye socket, but her mind didn't process it. She dug deeper, and animalistic screams rose above the chaos outside — both from her and from her would-be attacker.

Sidney yanked her hand free, the gelatinous orb came with it and she kicked him in the groin. When he doubled over, his optical nerve snapped wetly, leaving her with his eyeball grasped in her hand. He fell away, clutching at his ruined face and she advanced forward, kicking him in the throat. All those years of kickboxing technique were thrown out the window as she simply drew her foot back and kicked repeatedly, crushing his larynx.

He gurgled incoherently and she kicked again, this time missing the softer tissue and connecting with the bones of his cheek. The impact sent a jarring shudder up her leg that caused her stomach to seize in pain and brought her back to herself as she fell backward onto the air mattress.

The taste of copper was heavy in her mouth and her head throbbed in pain. She held something... She immediately flung the offensive thing toward the opening of her tent. That's when she noticed the form at her feet. The body of a male lay there, twitching slightly, but the movement seemed involuntary and sluggish. Outside, the sounds shouting, cries of pain, and the intermittent reports of gunfire carried across the camp and she remembered the riot.

She brought her hand up feel her forehead and saw blood covering her hand.

"What?"

She still couldn't remember what had happened. There was the riot, and then she hid behind the backpacks. She twisted slightly, feeling sore all over. The packs were where she remembered them being, so that wasn't any help.

Sidney felt gingerly along the skin of her forehead, stopping when they encountered a warm, wet fluid. She pushed gently and was rewarded with a sharp stab of pain.

A soft, gurgling exhalation of air brought her eyes to the man on the floor and everything came rushing back to her. The threats…the fight…the death of her attacker. Had she done that to him?

She pushed herself up tentatively. Her body was still a wreck from whatever had happened. It took a moment to gain her feet. When she did, she limped over to the body. His face was a purple, bloody mess. One eye was—

"Oh God," she moaned, remembering the squishy thing she'd been holding when her mind retook control. Sidney glanced at the small lump near the tent flap. She'd done that to him.

"No," she said aloud. "I stopped him from doing that to *me*."

Back to the body, she saw that it was indeed the same man who'd tried to attack her all those months ago. His face was burned in her memory and easily recognizable, even through the blood and discoloration. He'd threatened her baby and she'd obviously lost her mind. *Maybe I am crazy like everyone says*, she thought.

"Sidney!"

She snapped her head up and looked through the tent flap. A soldier ran toward her tent. She carried a rifle and three or four men kept pace behind her.

"Sidney! It's Caitlyn. Sidney!"

She hobbled forward to the edge of the tent and stuck a bloody hand outside. "In here," she croaked, her throat dry and parched.

Gravel skittered against the tent's fabric as Caitlyn came to a stop. "Oh God, Sidney. What happened?" she asked, looking inside at the carnage.

"He attacked. It...it was self-defense!" Sidney stammered, not knowing the intent of the soldiers behind Caitlyn.

Her friend stepped through the flap and surveyed the scene for a moment. "The riot's just about over," Caitlyn stated. "I was worried sick about you."

Sidney smiled and said, "I'm a—what was it you called me? A hard-nosed bitch?"

"Yeah," she replied and wrapped Sidney in a hug. The woman's tactical vest and rifle were painful against her chest, but she didn't care this time. It felt incredibly good to have physical contact with someone and she held on tightly.

After a few moments, one of the men outside cleared his throat, bringing the two of them back to the present. They broke off their embrace awkwardly and leaned away from one another.

"I was worried about you," Caitlyn began. "We got word that the riot started because a refugee was seen returning to the camp with a soldier carrying bags and boxes of food yesterday. I immediately thought of you since you had those two boxes and the bag of clothes."

Sidney nodded and pointed at the body. "He said the same thing. They thought I got food from the Army and wasn't sharing with anyone else."

Caitlyn nodded and glanced back at her soldiers outside. "Okay. Pack up your things. You're coming with me."

Sidney stepped back. "What?"

"No, you're not under arrest," Caitlyn clarified. "It's too dangerous here for you now. You have a target on your back and this will just keep happening until they kill you—or your baby."

That last part made Sidney realize that Caitlyn was right. She was already an outcast in the camp. If people thought she was getting preferential treatment... "How many people were hurt in the riot?"

"Too early to tell," Caitlyn replied. "There are a lot of bodies on the ground. A *lot*." She stared off to the side for a moment before continuing. "What do we need to do to get you ready to go?"

It didn't take the soldiers long to pack up her meager belongings. The hardest part was getting Rick James into the cat carrier, after that, it was over and done with in ten minutes. Sidney had debated just leaving the tent, but decided to take it, just in case. Everything went into her old Home Depot shopping cart and two of the men manhandled it over the gravel toward the camp perimeter.

"I hope you throw that bitch over the walls and let the infected eat her!" a small voice yelled. Sidney turned her head to find the source of the offensive comment. It was the little boy who'd called her the crazy cat lady the day before.

She started to reply, but Caitlyn pushed her onward. A crowd began to form along the gravel pathway. Many of the people had blood on their clothing. They yelled obscenities and gestured wildly in her direction. Several of them shouted their approval that the soldiers had arrested the *thief*.

"Better to let them think we're taking you into custody," Caitlyn muttered gruffly where only she could hear. "They'll never see you again after this. Hopefully, the entire thing will blow over and people will calm down."

By the time they'd covered the distance to where the riot began, Sidney doubted that the people of Camp Three would forget or let the aftermath of their actions blow over. She doubted it because of the bodies.

There were hundreds of them, maybe even thousands. They'd been packed in tightly around the trucks when the shooting started from both sides. Caught in the middle, they'd been unable to go anywhere and died in place, most of them from trampling. Sidney counted at least eight of the big Stryker vehicles that must have been called in for support. In addition to all the soldiers each vehicle carried, they also bristled with weapons that could be fired from inside. These people had died horribly, because of a misunderstanding.

No. The remaining refugees in Camp Three would never forget. She didn't know about the other camps inside the walls, but this one would be a problem from now on.

Sidney glanced furtively at Caitlyn's pretty face, covered with dust and specks of blood. *Where is she taking me?* she wondered. *Any place is better than this hellhole.*

8

MIDLAND-ODESSA, TEXAS
SEPTEMBER 15TH

Jake sighed contentedly. He'd eaten an entire can of baked beans. It was more food at one time than he'd had in months. The rationing had started almost immediately after the disaster was declared and since then, soldiers got two reduced-sized meals a day—which was still more than the average citizen. Over time, the meals had steadily gotten leaner and the soups more watered down.

"That hit the spot," he said, his eyes rolling to the side where Carmen watched him closely.

"I'm glad you liked it," she replied. "I know we don't have a lot to offer, but anything is better than nothing, right?"

"Yeah," he agreed and then changed his mind. "Wait, there's tons of stuff here."

"I mean variety," she amended. "We don't have a lot of variety. If we could have figured out a way to save the meat, then I could have whipped you up a proper meal."

He sat up quickly. "Are you kidding me?" he asked. "You don't need to apologize for not having power. The fact that you survived this long on your own is amazing."

"I'm ready to go," she replied. "I've been here too long with just my kids. I *need* adult interaction."

Jake eyed the Latina. She'd been wearing a t-shirt and shorts when they first arrived. Since then, she'd steadily shed layers of clothing. Now she wore a bikini top from the store's clothing section without a shirt and cutoff jeans. She said something about the rising temperatures inside, but he wasn't stupid. They both knew the game she was playing. Carmen was working her curves in an effort to save her kids' lives.

For their part, the two children ran around the store, going from soldier to soldier with curiosity.

They didn't ask for anything, like the refugee children at Fort Bliss did, they just seemed curious about other people. In awe that there were still normal humans alive.

"You've been here the whole time, alone?" he asked.

"Yes—well, there was another family here at first. They had the same idea as me, but the radio kept saying that there was a big safe zone set up in El Paso and they figured they could make it, so they packed up a car load of stuff and left."

"You know if they made it?"

She shrugged and shook her head. "No idea. So… Are your soldiers done loading those trailers yet? I'm real anxious to leave."

Jake set the empty can down on the floor and leaned forward. "Yeah. We're just about done. I think we'll be ready to head outside and begin the sling load soon."

The operation had taken longer than he'd thought it would. They'd planned for the possibility that it could take two full days to load the three trailers, but Jake hadn't thought that it would actually take that long. It had, though, because they had to unload two of them first. One had been full of heavy patio furniture. It was spring when the infection hit, so that made sense that the store would be full of that stuff, but the other truck made him scratch his head.

The truck was three-quarters full of all sorts of winter equipment, from snow blowers and heaters, to sleds and skiing equipment. He guessed that they'd been loading the truck to take it all back to some giant distribution centers somewhere when everything went to shit. And now, he'd inherited the problem. The furniture was heavy, but for the most part it was in boxes, ready to take home and assemble. The other stuff, especially the giant snow blowers, were bulky and hard to move without the use of a forklift. It had taken a team of fifteen soldiers just to disassemble the jigsaw puzzle-like packing job and empty the trailer.

"*Sir*," Jake's radio crackled to life on his vest.

He pulled it off and pressed the button. "This is Red One, over."

"*Hey, sir. It's Turner. We're starting to get a lot of curious infected in the area. The guys are making too much noise loading those trucks. The snipers are doing a hell of a job, but we need to speed this up before the sling load operation becomes too dangerous.*"

Jake waited for his platoon sergeant to finish his transmission with the proper radio procedures, but after a couple of seconds, he decided that the old

NCO wasn't going to, so he answered. "Alright. I'll talk to the guys, but I was thinking about it. When we send the teams outside, I want that sixth helicopter to fly as low as they can and lead the infected away again. Can you go talk to the pilots and let them know my idea? Over."

"Roger, sir."

"Fun time's over, Carmen," Jake said, pushing up from the camp chair he was sitting on.

She hopped up quickly and came over to him, placing a hand on his arm. "You're not gonna break your promise, are you, Jake? You'll take us with you?"

"Yes, ma'am," he replied, gently pushing her hand away before one of his men saw the gesture. "You don't need to worry about that. We'll take you with us to Fort Bliss. From there, they'll process you and you can decide between citizen or service."

She leaned in, more insistently than before. "Do I have to choose between the two? Before all of this, I was an ICU nurse, maybe I could work in the hospital or whatever is there. Or, can't we just stay with you?"

"Ha! The LT's picked up his own dependa," a voice called out from nearby, eliciting a chorus of laughs from the others.

"I share a room with two other lieutenants, Carmen. There's no room for you with me. I don't know about the medical center. Maybe."

"I heard about those refugee camps on the radio before it went dead," she replied. "They aren't a good place for a single woman to be, Jake. Can't you find *any* other option? I mean, you're an officer. All of these men listen to you…"

"If you don't get processed through the correct way, then you don't eat," he said. "And it's not like there's extra housing sitting around waiting for more refugees to arrive. We're practically bursting at the seams as it is."

She crossed her arms under her breasts. They pressed together and upward, making Jake wonder if the result of the movement was accidental or carefully practiced. "Then put my food back," she demanded.

"Excuse me?"

"You heard me. I was here first. Everything in the store is mine. Put it back and get out of here."

"We can't do that, Carmen. There are millions of refugees in Fort Bliss. Everything that's here will only last a day, maybe two if they're really creative, but it's something. This food has to go back."

"And it will last me and my kids for the rest of our lives," she replied coolly. "If you can't get me a place for my kids, *not* in the refugee camp, then I want all of *my* food put back and for you to leave before you bring all of the psychos from the city here."

"Ma'am, I—" He stopped. His authority as an officer extended to this situation because the president had declared martial law long ago. If he wanted to, he could simply take it from her and either leave her here or force her to go to the refugee camp; the former wasn't really an option, though. They'd cleaned out everything edible that they could find. Leaving her here with no food was a death sentence. Could he find someplace for her to stay? He supposed he could, but that set a dangerous precedence as he was sure that every warehouse they'd raid in the future would likely have people in them as well.

"What's it going to be, Jake? Are you taking me with you and not forcing me to join the Army, and not forcing me to go into the refugee tent city, or are you emptying those trucks and leaving my home?"

"I could just shoot you," Jake replied. "I could say that you were infected. Nobody would ever check."

"You wouldn't do that, though," she asserted, wide eyed.

"You don't know me very well, lady. I've killed hundreds of people. My men have killed thousands upon thousands. Don't threaten me."

He turned to storm off, but she grabbed his arm and whirled him around. "Don't you walk away from me, asshole. I'm talking to you."

He glared down at her. She was five-four, maybe five-five, and he was six-two. He towered over her, but she stood her ground, staring back at him, unafraid. He could easily end things, but... Jake threw up his hands. "Goddamn it. Fine. I'll find a way to get you a home on base, but you still have to process through the center or you won't get food."

"Don't try to double-cross me, Jake Murphy."

"I won't."

"If you do, I will find you and I'll make you wish you'd never even thought about doing that. Do you hear me?"

"Yeah, geez. I'll get you a place." He glanced over his shoulder to where all the men stood staring at their exchange. "Now, excuse me. I have to get these trucks loaded so we can get out of here."

"I mean it, Jake. I'm Puerto Rican," she called after him as he walked away. "I'll cut you if you screw me or my kids over."

He shook his head. What the hell had he just agreed to?

The rotor wash from the Chinook as it lifted off was enough to press Jake's face into the building's roof. It was go time. Now or never to test their concept of food resupply.

He'd ordered as many men as could fit, plus Carmen and her children, onto the first helicopter. It'd be the decoy bird to draw the infected away from the sling load operation. The remainder of the soldiers would pull security during the operation, loading into each helicopter before it went airborne to have a trailer hooked up to it. The sling load team, and the final security elements, would have to be hoisted up inside the last helicopter while they were in flight. It was that, or he could trust the crazy-assed pilot who assured him that he could hover near enough to the roof—with the trailer slung below—for the sling load team to jump onto the back ramp. He wasn't crazy about either option.

"You ready, sir?" Sergeant Turner yelled into his ear over the sound of the retreating helicopter.

"Yeah. Let's get this over with."

Jake stood and watched the first Chinook fly eastward for a few blocks before it stopped, then lowered slowly toward the ground. The gunners began to fire almost immediately and he ducked his head, running toward the hole in the roof.

He sat and swung his legs over the edge before turning onto his stomach. "You got it, sir," a soldier called from below. "Just reach with your left foot... Got it!"

His foot touched the top of the ladder and he gently eased his weight onto the step. When it held, he risked a glance past his body. The outline of the ladder stretched into the gloom below. It only took a few seconds for him to descend the ladder.

Then he was running with the other soldier toward the loading docks in back. When he got there, four more soldiers waited. They already wore heavy gloves and the oversized dust goggles that they'd been issued back at Bliss.

"Ready, sir?" an NCO from Mirman's platoon asked.

Jake eyed the 101st Airborne patch on his shoulder. "You sure you got this, Sergeant Orroro?"

"Done it hundreds of times, sir. I just had a shitty assignment manager who made me leave Fort Campbell last year."

Jake slapped him on the shoulder. "Be thankful he did, otherwise you'd be dead!" He put his own goggles on and one of the gloves before grabbing the radio strapped onto his vest. "Sergeant Turner, this is Red One. Over."

"Go ahead, sir."

"We're in position at the back door. Did you guys drop the chains? Over."

"Yes, sir. Each trailer has four or five chains on the roof. A couple of them fell off. Nothing we can do about those."

"Okay. Give me the word when it's safe for us to go outside."

The old NCO paused for a moment and Jake took the opportunity to pull on his other glove. *"You're good to go, sir. The loading dock is clear."*

Jake depressed the horizontal door bar and pushed, leading the way out onto the three-foot wide concrete loading dock. It was the first time any of them had been out there; the trailers had been married up to their doors already when they arrived. The stench of rotten meat was overwhelming outside. This is where Carmen and the other family had dumped all of the meat from inside once the power to the refrigerators and freezers went out.

"Oh, God. That's awful," the soldier right behind him said, gagging.

"It's not as bad over by the trucks," Jake whispered. "Just get over there."

Sergeant Orroro held the door for the two men carrying a long ladder. They had to get it in place and then get up on top of the trailer before any infected showed up. The two men ran until they were beside the trailer and they opened the ladder.

Jake followed behind and then stopped when he saw the body. A badly decomposed form, about the size of a male, was only a few feet from the dock. He'd been stabbed through the eye—the handle of a screwdriver blade protruded from the eye socket. "Who the fuck is that?" he asked.

"Who cares," Orroro said, pushing past him. "Let's go, sir. You don't want to be down here when we start moving those chains around."

The six of them scrambled up the ladder quickly and Jake looked up at Sergeant Turner, ten feet above him. "Still clear, sir," Turner whispered, giving him a thumbs up.

They worked quickly, as rehearsed. While Jake went to the end of the trailer to watch for infected,

Orroro's team went to each corner and began to feed the massive chains that the soldiers above had dropped onto the roofs through the eyelets welded into the trailer. The sixth soldier busied himself with moving the ladder from one side of the trailer to the other. Once this one was ready to go, they'd have to climb down and then move over to the next trailer ten feet away.

The worst part was that they'd have to repeat the up and down process backward once the helicopters were hovering overhead.

The chains made more noise than Jake would have imagined possible. The men tried their best to lessen the noise, but there was nothing they could do to stop the clanging of the metal links against the trailer's eyelets. Once the corners were in and a large pin ran through the links to keep them bound together, the four soldiers dragged the running end of their chains to more or less the center of the roof where Orroro connected them together onto a massive U-shaped shackle and secured it with the safety pin.

The sergeant set the shackle down carefully, ensuring that the chains weren't twisted and then said, "Okay. This one's ready."

Jake nodded. "Let's go over to the next one."

They didn't see any infected until they were hooking the chains into the shackle on the fifth and final trailer.

"Shit!' Jake cursed, raising his weapon and firing at the creature as it rounded the corner. The report was much louder than the clinking of the chains had been. He snatched the radio off his chest angrily. "Where did that guy come from?"

"We didn't see him up here," Sergeant Turner asserted.

"Well he came from some—"

Another infected appeared at roughly the same spot. It came slowly at first, then began to scream and ran toward the trailers when it saw the six men up high. It dropped with a hole in its head.

"Sniper got that one, sir. He thinks there's a hole in a fence or something out of our line of sight that they're coming through."

"We're ready to go. Get the birds up and going," Jake said into the radio.

The NCO didn't reply. Instead, less than thirty seconds later, the engines of the helicopters roared to life and the whine of the blades beginning to turn echoed across the loading dock.

That's when Jake heard more of the screams. He turned in a full circle, trying to determine where they came from before the rotors spun up to full speed and drowned out all noise. The best he could tell, they were on the other side of a concrete wall about a hundred feet away.

Another infected appeared at the corner of the building, and then another immediately on its heels. Both went down, only to be replaced by more of them streaming in from somewhere. He aimed and fired, hitting one as it was already falling from the snipers' bullets overhead.

"You've got far, we'll get near!" he shouted into the radio.

"*Acknowledged. Good luck, sir,*" Turner's voice came back.

The loading dock fell into shadow as the first Chinook lifted off, then lowered carefully over them. Jake risked a look up at the bird. The crew chief's masked face appeared through a small square opening in the bottom of the helicopter. He was talking the pilots into position over the trailer and the four-man team holding the chains.

Jake turned back around and fired at one of the infected that was less than twenty feet away, well inside the snipers' field of view so they wouldn't be able to engage it. He hit the woman high on the shoulder, spinning her around, but she quickly turned back and continued toward him. He took a half second to settle his nerves and lined up on the woman's forehead. What was left of her hair flew wildly as the back of her skull exploded out behind her. She dropped instantly and Jake had to take a knee because the rotor wash from above practically knocked him over.

The snipers continued firing at targets and for the moment, the lieutenant's engagement area was clear. He looked at the team behind him. Sergeant Orroro had the massive shackle in his hands while another soldier used a long pole to tap at the pintle hook underneath the Chinook, discharging the static electricity that could kill the man hooking the chains to the bird.

Jake turned back to scan his area. Nothing was close, but there was a low mound of dead infected near the corner of the building. He glanced in the opposite direction—everyone on the roof was probably focused on killing the creatures in front of him, so he wanted to be sure that nothing was coming from behind the team around the opposite side of the building.

It was clear, and so was the sling load team. The helicopter lifted slowly, taking the slack out of the chains and easing the pressure of the rotor wash.

When the chains were fully extended, Sergeant Orroro checked them one more time for kinks or twists and then gave the crew chief a thumbs up.

Then the race was on. They ran to the back of the trailer and went down the ladder rapidly. Jake didn't like that they were only four feet off the ground on the small ledge; a mob of infected could easily reach them, but it was what it was.

Once everyone was off the roof, the soldier in charge of the ladder moved it to the other trailer and held it in place while they all went up, and then followed them up himself. Jake waved the first helicopter away and it lifted skyward, the chains groaning as they adjusted to the weight. In seconds, the bird was away and flying westward toward Fort Bliss.

"There's one!" Jake yelled enthusiastically as he went to the end of the trailer so the men could work with him out of the way.

"Son of a bitch!" Several of the infected had made it past the snipers and were also out of Sergeant Turner's line of sight. Jake fired point blank into their faces, sending them to hell—or wherever they went.

The next helicopter roared in and they were complete with the hook up in under five minutes. Trailers three and four went about the same as the first two, except that the infected had surprised him much quicker during the time it took to transition to the top of the fourth trailer as the sling load team got closer to the corner of the building.

Jake switched magazines again and congratulated himself for getting four of the five trailers of food secured. Then things went south during the transition to the last trailer. One of the infected had somehow made it past Jake unnoticed and grabbed Orroro's pant leg as he came down the ladder. The damned thing was screaming, but the hovering helicopter hooked to the container drowned out all sound.

Orroro stumbled and fell off the dock, nearly taking the ladder with him. The infected was on him in an instant, tearing at his face with desiccated fingers and biting. The sergeant fired his pistol three times and the infected rolled away, dead. He stood shakily and held up his hand to see. The large, jagged semi-circle of missing flesh on his wrist where the gloves ended and his uniform didn't reach told everyone all they needed to know.

"Mother fucker!" Orroro cursed. "I should have fucking stayed at Campbell. *Goddammit!*"

"Get up here, Sergeant," Jake ordered, leaning down to help pull him up. The NCO cursed loudly and punched the trailer. "Stop it. You may be immune," Jake stated. "The docs think that one-to-two percent of the population may be. Don't give up."

Orroro looked up at him and shook his head. "No, sir. I ain't got that kind of luck."

It took some work, but they got him up onto the loading dock and then scrambled back up the ladder onto the third trailer. The Chinook finally lifted away and turned west.

Jake slapped Orroro on the shoulder and went out to the end of the trailer. Behind him, the men worked quickly, preparing for the final helicopter.

The hook up was much slower this time as Orroro missed the pintle several times and the bird had to readjust. Once it was finally on, they waited for the chains to straighten and Jake had to verify that they were okay because the sergeant was crying.

"I'm done for, sir. I can already feel it moving inside me."

"That's in your head, man," Jake shouted over the rotors. "It doesn't move that fast."

Orroro shook his head violently. "I can *feel* it. I'm gonna turn." He wiped his eyes with his hand and then grimaced as blood from his wrist got into one of his eyes. "Fuck."

They climbed down the ladder, careful to avoid the spot where the sergeant's blood had smeared on one of the rungs. When they reached the bottom, they sprinted for the door and hurried inside the warehouse.

"I ain't no bitch, sir," Orroro said, seeming to have come to terms with his fate. "Gimme your grenades."

"Sergeant—"

"No, sir. I'll go out there and fuck as many of those things up as I can."

Jake nodded and stepped back. "Here," Orroro mumbled. "Here's my weapon and all my extra magazines. I know they keep telling us we're good, but we have to be running low on ammo. Brass never tell the grunts the truth."

He handed the soldiers everything he could that didn't have blood on it and then saluted Jake carefully to avoid flinging blood all over the lieutenant.

"Give 'em hell, Sergeant."

"Fuck those creeps, sir," the big man replied and then pushed his way out the door. "Now go!" Jake saw him hop down off the loading dock right before the door slammed shut.

The sling load team didn't wait any longer. They ran through the warehouse and then up the ladder to the roof. "Let's go!" Turner shouted as they emerged one by one through the skylight.

Jake ran to the edge of the building where the Chinook's back ramp hovered mere inches above the concrete. "We got everybody, Sergeant Turner?" he screamed over the noise of the engines.

"Yes, sir. You and me are the last ones, minus Sergeant Orroro."

Jake nodded and jumped up onto the ramp after Turner. The gunner waited until he was past him and then raised the ramp slightly, holding his hand over his mouth.

The engine noise changed and Jake felt the bird begin to elevate slowly. The roof dropped away below them and the pilot turned the nose westward.

He watched until the city was far behind them, but Jake never saw a cloud of dust or debris that would have indicated that Orroro detonated the grenades.

9

FORT BLISS MAIN CANTONMENT AREA, EL PASO, TEXAS
SEPTEMBER 15TH

"Well, this is all I can offer you," Caitlyn said with a lopsided grin. "It's not much, but until we can get someone from the garrison command to assign you different quarters, you'll have to bunk with me."

Sidney looked around the small room, barely more than a closet with a bunk bed and two wall lockers. The sheets on both beds were rumpled, so she guessed that someone else lived in the room as well, which made sense given how many people were crammed onto the installation. Most of the refugees in Camp Three were forced to do what the

Army called 'hot bunking' where one person would sleep for eight hours on the cot and then a different person would use the same cot to sleep a different shift.

To Sidney, the idea of four solid walls, regardless of where they were, was heaven. "Thank you, Caitlyn," she replied. "This is more than I ever imagined. You've been so nice, I—"

"Ah! None of that. You're here because you deserve to be." Her eyes visually went up and then down Sidney, causing her heart to beat a little faster. "You're filthy, girl. Let's get those off of you and we'll put them in my wash bag. Our laundry services are really good—but they tend to shrink stuff because of the hot water."

"Laundry service?" Sidney asked in amazement. All the refugees had were big basins of water and bar soap to scrub their clothing.

"Yeah. The Brass says that the smoke from burning infected, and certainly the blood if we come into contact with it, carries the disease, so they're super strict about ensuring we keep our clothes clean. We have three or four laundry and bath companies that work twenty-four-seven."

"The smoke carries the disease?" Sidney asked in alarm. "But all that ash and soot falls onto the refugee camps. It's all over everything. The food, the water…"

Caitlyn shrugged. "Yeah, I think it's garbage. Fire kills everything, right? I think it's more that they want us clean to avoid other diseases, but who knows. What's important is that you're here now, so let's get your clothing washed and get you a shower."

Sidney tried to remember what day of the week it was, and failed. "I can't remember what day it is."

"Monday."

"Okay, so Mondays are our shower days. What about the meal?"

"Sidney, you're on the Main Cantonment now. We can shower any time we want, not just one day a week. Ration issue is by my military ID, two times a day at the cafeteria. I can share my food with you for a day or so, but we'll definitely need to get you processed through Garrison so they can get you a ration card too."

The floor seemed to drop out from underneath Sidney's feet. She could shower whenever she wanted to? Like the walls, that fact seemed like heaven to her. She'd been forced to live amongst so many people for so long that she'd forgotten how little things like cleanliness—or the thought of being clean at this point—could make a person feel like a human once more.

"Are you okay?" Caitlyn asked.

"Yeah, I just—" She sighed, trying not to cry. "I'm just very thankful that I met you."

"Come here," the soldier ordered, pulling her into a hug. "It'll be okay." She disengaged and wrinkled her nose. "You've got that guy's blood all over you. Let's get those clothes off of you, and any of your other stuff that needs to be washed. While you're showering, I'll run everything over to the laundry, then first thing tomorrow morning, you'll have all clean clothes."

Sidney glanced down at her clothing in embarrassment. The new sweatpants and shirt that she'd just put on that morning were covered in blood—both her own and from the man who'd attacked her. "I'm kind of a mess, huh?"

"You could say that," Caitlyn agreed. "Here, let me help you."

The soldier bent down and untied her shoes for her, gently sliding them off, and then pulled her socks off as well. She tossed those into a thick, green pillowcase and then gently pulled Sidney's sweat pants off.

"Whoa. Um, do you need to borrow a razor, or is that how you always…"

Sidney felt her face redden. It'd been months since she shaved her legs. *Months*. "We couldn't get them out in the camp."

Caitlyn nodded and helped her step out of the pants without falling. "Well, don't worry. We have some here. I can get you shaving cream and a razor." She stood up and gestured toward the shirt. "That too. It's disgusting."

She did as directed and felt her breasts flop downward as they came free of the shirt. It was definitely an odd feeling for someone who'd lived her entire life with small boobs. With the pregnancy, her A cup had ballooned to a solid B, maybe even a C if she lied to herself.

"We'll have to get the doc up here to look at you, get you on a proper diet and everything. *Oh!*" she exclaimed, making Sidney, now nude and self-conscious, jump slightly. "Sorry. Maybe the doctor can prescribe you extra rations too. That'd be good."

"The doctor that I saw once down at the camp gave me a couple extra ration tickets, but it wasn't much."

Caitlyn turned away and rummaged inside the leftmost wall locker. "Well, things run differently over here, so… Here you go," she said, turning around, holding a razor, can of cream, a new box of bar soap, and a washcloth.

"Wow. You're…"

"Efficient. I know. It's one of my stellar qualities." She smirked and pulled a towel down off the back of the door. "Here's my towel. Let me warn you though: it's the standard, Army brown, water resistant towel, so you'll be more frustrated than dry by the end of things."

Sidney laughed. "Oh, it can't be that bad."

"Worse," Caitlyn deadpanned. "Come on. I'll show you to the showers. There's shampoo and conditioner in the dispensers on the stall wall that get refilled regularly. If yours is empty, just ask the person next to you for some."

She wrapped the towel around her body and followed behind the soldier. "So, this is the barracks for Able Company, 1st of the 36th Infantry. Not too exciting, I know, but it's home."

Sidney looked around dutifully, but wasn't too impressed. It looked just like any other hallway with rooms on each side. "First and most of Second Platoon are out on a big mission right now, so the place is fairly empty," Caitlyn told her. "They're supposed to be back sometime today, though, so get in there and get that shower before everyone comes back and all the guys start hitting on you."

"Guys?"

Caitlyn stopped. "Oh shit. I forgot to tell you."

"Tell me what?" Sidney asked, dreading the answer. Her mind immediately went to thinking that she was going to be forced to be some type of indentured prostitute for the Army men in return for her room and board.

"There are only five women in Able Company. We're all in the Third Platoon, but with so many more males, there's no way they could establish segregated showers or bathrooms. Is that going to be a problem?"

"Uh…" Even in the refugee camp, the bath and shower schedules were strictly enforced. "Have you had any problems?"

"Besides the occasional hard on from a nineteen year old as he ogles my body, no." She leaned in closer, "It's kind of fun. You get to frustrate the hell out of them and you have your pick of the group for when you need a little sexual release."

"Oh, uh… I don't think I'll be needing any sexual release."

Caitlyn shrugged. "You're a better woman than I am, Sidney."

They continued toward the showers. There wasn't a door on the room, just a large, open doorway. Sidney could already feel the humidity coming off the running showers inside. Caitlyn popped her head in and looked left.

"Hey, Dickerson," she said. "I've got Sidney, that refugee we brought over here with us. Make sure nobody fucks with her or I'll cut your dick off. Got it?"

"Yes, Sergeant," a male voice echoed from inside.

Caitlyn returned to the hallway. "Okay, Private Dickerson's in the shower now. He's the big guy from Kentucky who helped pack up your tent. Don't worry, he's harmless. He'll look out for you while I take your things over to the laundry. Then I have to stop by the company to make a sworn statement to the commander about my squad's actions during the riot."

"A sworn statement? Are you in trouble?"

"No. It's just standard procedure. Every squad leader that responded is being asked to provide one in case there's some type of investigation after all of this is over."

"All of this?"

"The infected," Caitlyn replied. "They aren't going to live forever. Then we'll be responsible for rebuilding the US."

"You think that's possible? I mean, can we come back from all of this?"

"Yeah. I think so. There's already talk about some government assistance along the West Coast. China or Japan or something like that sent some troops to help out. It's only a matter of time."

"China?"

"I don't know, maybe it was South Korea. It's all third- and fourth-hand knowledge from one of the base radio guys that I've been seeing." She shifted out of the doorway. "So, like I said, I'll be back in about twenty or thirty minutes, okay?"

"Okay," Sidney mumbled, feeling oddly apprehensive, like a kid being dropped off for summer camp for the first time.

"You remember which room is mine?"

"324."

"That's right. See you soon." Caitlyn leaned in and gave her a kiss on the cheek, then walked back down the hallway toward her room.

Sidney stood in the hallway for a moment, and then stepped inside. To the left was the bathroom, with several stalls and urinals, along with a double row of sinks. Immediately to the right was a small, open room with benches where people could dry off and get dressed. Beyond that were the showers. Directly along her line of vision was the soldier Caitlyn had mentioned. Was it Dickerson?

Oh shit! she groaned internally. She'd immediately looked at his crotch when she thought of his name.

She swallowed her pride and walked to the right. There was one towel hanging from a hook above a bench, so she unwrapped Caitlyn's towel and hung it up a few hooks down from his. She straightened her shoulders and gave herself a pep talk.

You can do this. You are a sexy, confident woman. It's just nudity. You've been naked in front of lots of people.

The last part, for good or bad, was true and she grabbed the thought and held on to it as she walked back toward the shower holding all of the items that Caitlyn had given her.

"Nice tats," Dickerson said. Her hands flew upward, covering her breasts. He laughed. "I said *tats*. You know, tattoos?"

"Uh, thanks," she replied, smiling in embarrassment as she sat her things on the little wire ledge screwed into the tile.

"I'm Eric. Nice to meet you, ma'am," the soldier said from close behind her, startling her.

She turned quickly, her stomach protesting the quick movement, and saw him only a couple of feet behind her with his hand outstretched.

"Ah…"

His smile faltered and he dropped his hand. "I'm sorry, ma'am. I didn't mean to scare you. It's just that we weren't introduced before."

Sidney tried to put aside her inhibitions about her new surroundings. She forced a smile and reached out. "Sorry. This is all so new to me. I'm Sidney."

He shook her hand gently before letting it drop. "I'm in Sergeant Wyatt's squad. Anything you need, let me know. Okay?"

She nodded shyly and turned back to the wall to turn on the water. As she stood to the side, adjusting the temperature, she risked a quick, furtive glance toward Dickerson. His penis was just a little bigger than it had been when she first came into the room.

She laughed out loud and stepped under the water.

"What?" the young soldier asked. "I know. My dad was a huge football fan."

"What?" she mimicked, confused.

"Eric Dickerson," he said. "Go ahead, I've heard it all."

"I don't know who that is," she admitted.

"Eric Dickerson? NFL running back? He holds the single season rushing record?"

"Nope," she laughed, raising her arms up to work the water into her hair so she could wash it."

"Oh, come on!" he said. "How do you not know who he is?"

"I'm not that big into sports, sorry."

"That's sacrilege, ma'am," he said, scrubbing between his ass cheeks.

Sidney glanced down at her feet, the water was a ruddy brown color, reminding her that she was covered in blood and ash from the burning infected. She wondered if the ash drifted this far from the walls.

Dickerson finished showering a few minutes later and walked by her. "I'm gonna wait out here in the latrine for you, ma'am. Sergeant Wyatt wanted me to make sure that nobody bothered you on your first day."

"You don't have to do that."

"Oh yes I do. She'll beat the shit out of me if anything happens while I'm supposed to be watching after you. She doesn't mess around."

"Okay. I'm warning you, though, I'm going to be a while. I haven't shaved my legs in about four months."

"It's okay, ma'am. I don't have anywhere to be until 0600 tomorrow when we go out to the wall."

Sidney nodded, noticing the man's eyes lingering on her body for a moment too long. "See everything you needed to, Eric Dickerson?"

"Uh… I'm sorry, ma'am," he rushed over his words. "I'll be right out here."

He disappeared around the corner and she laughed aloud once more. She was actually starting to feel like a human again. Even though the setting and the circumstances were *odd*, she enjoyed interacting with other people who weren't watching her warily, waiting for her guard to drop so they could take whatever it was that she had.

Plus, Private Dickerson had been easy on the eyes.

True to his word, Dickerson was waiting in the small dressing room with only a pair of boxer shorts on, holding his towel. She acknowledged him with a slight nod as she walked by, naked and dripping wet.

"Feel better, ma'am?" he asked, doing his best to look at the floor.

"Much better, thank you."

She struggled with the brown towel to dry off. Just as Caitlyn had warned her, the damn thing resisted water and worked more like a squeegee to push the water around than to absorb it. It was truly a marvel of modern manufacturing failure. After what seemed like hours of twisting, turning, and stretching to reach all the crevices on her body, she was dry enough to wrap the towel around herself.

"All done," she announced, noticing the obvious bulge in Dickerson's shorts after her show.

"Okay, ma'am. Just in time, too. It sounds like the other platoons got back from their mission."

He stood and led the way, holding his towel low in front of his crotch. She followed him to the hallway. "I'm this way," he said, pointing toward the opposite direction. "Room 301 if you need anything."

"Oh, okay. I'm staying down with Cait— With Sergeant Wyatt." He nodded and went toward his room.

Sidney walked down the hallway as a large group of men came in, fully geared up for combat. Several of them gave her the once over as she walked barefoot, covered only in a towel, toward her new room.

When she was almost there, she noticed a face that looked familiar. "Hey, I know you," she said. "You were the medic that checked me out when I came to the city."

"I'd like to check you out," he laughed, high-fiving several of his buddies.

"Real mature, Specialist Mitchell," Caitlyn said from her doorway. "This is Sidney. She's under my direct supervision. Anyone caught fucking with her will have to answer to me. Got it?"

"Yes, Sergeant," the medic replied. Several nearby soldiers replied in the affirmative as well.

"Good. She's gonna be staying here for a few days. Treat her like a member of Able Company and we won't have any problems."

Sidney hurried down the hall and slipped into Caitlyn's room where she dug through the plastic bag of clothing she'd gotten from the PX yesterday. As she changed, the soldier stood in the doorway talking to a Hispanic male NCO.

"Were you guys successful?" she asked.

"Yeah, we got five full trailers of food and medicine. Cleaned the place out, and even had room for some other shit like cigarettes, a bunch of folding camp chairs, sunscreen, and bug juice."

"The LT say how long that stuff will last?"

"Nah," the guy replied, "but you know him. He wants everyone to believe that it'll be okay, so he won't say anything."

She nodded and glanced over her shoulder at Sidney and smiled. Then she turned back around. "There are too many people here, Gallegos. It's not sustainable."

"I heard you guys took care of some of that problem today."

Caitlyn shook her head. "It was disgusting, man. They were rioting and shooting at the Civilian Division troopers bringing them food. We got the order to put it down."

"How many?" Sergeant Gallegos asked.

She shrugged. "Early estimates are—" She stopped and looked back at Sidney again. "Estimates are pretty high. The commander thinks maybe as many as ten thousand. There was a lot of lead flying in both directions."

Sidney's vision began to go black at the edges and she got light headed. She stumbled backward and had to sit on the bottom bunk.

"Are you okay?" Caitlyn asked. Somehow she was kneeling right in front of Sidney.

"I, uh... Yeah. I thought I heard you say ten thousand refugees were dead."

Caitlyn's lips thinned. "They didn't stop fighting us, even after we shot into the crowd with small arms. They didn't begin dispersing until we opened fire with the Bushmasters."

"What's that?"

"The big gun on top of the Strykers. It tore through them. Sidney, it was horrible."

"And you killed ten thousand of them? Of *us*?" she accused.

"No. Most of the deaths occurred from people trampling one another." She shuddered and then sighed. "It was so stupid. Over food."

Sidney remembered what her attacker said. They'd rioted over seeing her with bags of clothing and thought it was food. In effect, *she'd* killed all those people.

"I... I need to lie down for a little while," Sidney said.

"Of course." Caitlyn stood and stepped back. "I'm gonna go get cleaned up. Don't freak out if that guy I was talking to, Staff Sergeant Gallegos, comes in here. He's on the top bunk."

"Your roommate is a guy?"

"Being an NCO comes with a few perks, like this massive room for just the two of us," Caitlyn said, holding her arms wide and then pulling her shirt off.

"He doesn't think it's weird when you, ah, release your sexual tension with one of the guys?"

"Well, so far, he's never been in the room. He's in First Platoon and we usually have different schedules."

"Oh." Sidney's eyelids were drooping as the day's events caught up with her. "Where should I set up my mattress?"

"No such luck," Caitlyn replied, fully nude now. "There was a big hole cut in it from that kitchen knife. Until we can get it repaired, you and me are gonna have to share the bed. You okay with that?"

Sidney nodded and lay back as Caitlyn came over to her and pulled the sheet and blanket out from under her body. She noticed dreamily that the soldier's body was just as she'd imagined it would be: firm, pale, and visually appealing.

"When Gallegos gets undressed, don't freak out."

"Why?" she muttered, already falling into sleep.

"Because that fucker's got a giant cock. Scared the shit out of me the first time I saw it, thought he had an infection or something."

Caitlyn laughed and grabbed her wet towel from behind the door. Just before she fell asleep, she heard Gallegos say, "Yeah, real funny, bitch."

"We all love you, buddy," Caitlyn replied.

10

FORT BLISS MAIN CANTONMENT AREA, EL PASO, TEXAS
SEPTEMBER 16TH

"Shit, son. You did it."

"Thank you, sir."

"To be honest, I didn't think it would work. There's so many of those damned things out there that I figured you guys would have to abort."

Jake swallowed the lump that had risen in his throat when the division commander, Major General Bhagat, complimented him. Now, the praise seemed tarnished, lessened by the older man's admission that he didn't have any faith in Jake and his men. *What a crock of shit.*

"I was confident that it would work, sir," Colonel Albrecht, the 1st Stryker Brigade commander, stated. "Lieutenant Murphy is one of the Ready First Brigade's most able and adaptable leaders—that's why I assigned it to his battalion. I knew it would filter down to him and he'd make this thing work."

The general nodded at the colonel. "Thanks, Jim." He turned back to Jake and held out his hand. Grasped between his fingers was a triangular coin, painted yellow, blue, and red with a bold number "**1**" emblazoned above a cannon with tank treads and a red lightning bolt over the top of it. At the bottom, the words "**OLD IRONSIDES**" denoted the First Armored Division patch. "Here you go, Lieutenant Murphy. It's not much, but it'll have to do for now. I'm sure that somebody will write you up for an actual award soon, and since I'm the highest ranking Army officer on the installation—hell, possibly in the entire western half of the United States at this point—I'm pretty sure I'll approve it."

He winked and Jake took the coin from him. "Thank you, sir."

"That food will go a long way toward helping people eat, Lieutenant. You did good."

"I barely had anything to do with it, sir. My men were—"

"Can it, son. I've already been told that you led the team down on the ground and about your soldier who was killed. That could have just as easily been you, so don't go saying that you didn't put yourself at risk."

"Yes, sir," Jake replied dumbly. He'd had a lot of time to think about Sergeant Orroro's death and he'd never even once considered that he could have been bitten.

"Now, you go tell your soldiers that Iron Six personally told you that I'm proud of them."

"Yes, sir."

The general looked down at a stack of papers in front of him and then back up at the two men. "Alright, sir. Thank you for taking time out of your busy day to meet Lieutenant Murphy," Colonel Albrecht said.

"No problem, Jim. I want to talk to you about a few more operations that my planners think are within range, and about that riot in your sector yesterday."

"My staff is preparing a full report, sir. I—"

"Forget it, Jim." The general stopped and looked at Jake. "Good job, Lieutenant. Go back to your platoon. I'm sure you've got a mission coming up soon."

Jake nodded and saluted, which the general returned. "Hey, Jake," Colonel Albrecht called as he wheeled around. "Come see me at 1700, I want to get a quick debrief. No slides or any of that crap, just talk to me, okay?"

"Yes, sir."

He wheeled back around and walked stiffly toward the door. Behind him, he heard the general say, "Damnedest thing, that riot. On one hand, it's a tragedy. On the other, it's a godsend. Ten thousand less mouths to feed."

"Actually, sir, the new estimates put it closer to twenty thousand."

"Damn," the general said. "Now, *that* will make that food go a lot farther…"

Jake didn't hear the rest of the conversation as the general's aide closed the door behind him. Iron Six was right. It was a tragedy that so many people lost their lives, but that meant that fewer people eating the dwindling food supplies. In all honesty, out of a four million-refugee population, it wasn't even that many people, but it would help.

"Oh my God," Jake chastised himself as he took the stairs to the first floor. "I can't believe that I just thought that the death of innocent civilians was a good thing."

They obviously weren't all innocent, he told himself, referring to the instigators and the aggressors in the crowd who'd fired on the soldiers. The Third Platoon had lost two dead and a bunch of wounded, but the Civilian Division had taken a pounding. He hadn't seen official reports yet, but his roommate, Joe, said they'd had over a hundred people killed. They'd been right in the thick of things delivering the rations when the riot turned deadly.

He walked across the entryway, his boots squeaking annoyingly on the tile floor. He'd always hated coming over to the division headquarters, even more so now when compared to the conditions in the refugee camps. While those people lived in terrible, overcrowded conditions, this big building was unoccupied except for staff, and was always kept spotless. It could probably hold five thousand people, maybe more.

And then his thoughts from the stairwell hit him, hard enough this time that he paused for a moment before continuing through the glass doors to the outside. Even if the headquarters building were opened up and *ten thousand* people were able to move into it to get out of Tent City, it wouldn't even make a dent in the population out there.

Four million. There were four million refugees crammed inside the walls of Fort Bliss. Four million mouths to feed, every day. It was a losing battle. The food runs were only delaying the inevitable. The land inside the base wasn't good for crop farming, even if they could find enough of it to do anything with. They *would* run out of food sooner or later and then, what? Cannibalism? What else could that many people do for food? When people are hungry enough, they'll do some crazy shit.

"It's a losing battle," Jake mumbled, repeating what he'd just thought. "My men are going to keep risking their lives to fight a losing battle."

For the first time in his career, Jake considered giving up. He could take off his uniform and melt into the camps, lie down and give up like everyone else and wait for the inevitable end to come.

It was an interesting prospect, but it wasn't who he was. He would fight and in all likelihood, die for the people in those camps. "No," he continued, eliciting stares from passersby. "I'll stick around, and we'll make this thing work."

"I remember you," Sidney told the officer sitting at the table beside her. When he'd sat down at the dining hall table beside her and Caitlyn, it took her a moment to remember why he looked familiar, but she was good with faces and recognized where she'd seen him before.

"Excuse me?" the man replied.

"You were on the checkpoint…was it Checkpoint Fox? The first line of defense around the city back in the old days."

"Foxtrot."

"Yeah, that's it," she said. "You were the guy in charge out there when I came through."

He shrugged. "I was out there for almost a month. Did you, ah…" he stared pointedly at her stomach. "Did you decide to join the Civilian Division, then?"

"No, I was in the refugee camp until yesterday."

"What she means, sir," Caitlyn interjected quickly, "is that she would have joined the CD if they would have let her, but since she's pregnant, they wouldn't."

Lieutenant Murphy glanced at the NCO and then back at Sidney. "So, what are you doing here on the Main Cantonment, eating in the soldiers' dining hall?"

"We got her permission—"

The lieutenant held up his hand, indicating that Caitlyn needed to stop talking. "I asked her, Sergeant. Not you."

Sidney picked up her napkin and began to twist it. "I'm here because I was the cause of the food riot yesterday at Camp Three, the one that all those people died at."

He set his fork down. "Go on."

"A few days ago, I tried to come over here to see if there were any clothes for me. Everything I had with me when I arrived was for a size zero, and obviously," she leaned back and patted her belly, "I can't wear it anymore. There aren't any supplies available for refugees."

He rolled his hand, indicating that she should continue . "And?"

"And Caitlyn—Staff Sergeant Wyatt—stopped me and offered to help."

"Is that right?" He looked pointedly at Caitlyn.

"Yes, sir," she answered. "It isn't against the regs to allow a refugee escorted access to the Main Post."

"I know it's not. Hell, half of my platoon has dated a camp woman, but—"

"A *what*?" Sidney hissed.

The lieutenant held up his hands. "I'm sorry, ma'am. I didn't mean any offense. I meant to say that people *are* allowed to go back and forth with an escort, but I've never heard of anyone getting clothing from Supply. Is that even legal?"

"It wasn't from the Supply Sergeant, sir," Caitlyn continued. "I took her to the PX and she bought a few pairs of sweat pants and tank tops with cash."

"*Hmpf,*" he snorted. "I don't know why they bother with taking cash anymore. It's worthless."

"Well, I'm glad they did," Sidney said. "Otherwise I'd be screwed."

He shrugged and took a bite of meat that the menu said was beef, but she wasn't sure where they'd have gotten it, unless those helicopters flying all over the place were just ferrying food from massive warehouses somewhere. "So, how did *you* start the riot?"

"People saw me with bags of clothes, a box of diapers, and a car seat. They jumped to conclusions, accusing me of getting food that wasn't available to them, and…" She trailed off purposefully.

"Yeah, I know," he laughed. "It doesn't make any sense, but in a way, it makes perfect sense. Even the soldier's diet has shrunk by an entire meal, and the portion sizes are easily half of what they were on day one. And we're expected to go out there and fight every day. I can't imagine what they're giving the refugees."

"One meal a day, smaller than this one here," Sidney pointed at her tray on the table in front of her. "Nobody's dying of starvation that I know of, but it isn't pretty over there. People get attacked for scraps of food all the time."

"I wish there was something we could do," Lieutenant Murphy replied. "I really do. To be honest, we never thought this many of the infected would come to the desert or that they'd be able to survive this long. As far as I know, Fort Bliss and El Paso were supposed to be a temporary solution, a few months at most while the infected died out."

"All your smarty-pants planners didn't ask anyone on the run from those things, did they?" Sidney grunted.

"What do you mean?"

"Those things out there just followed the sights and sounds. At first, it was the lines of cars, coming from all over the nation to one place. Then it was the sounds of helicopters taking off, planes flying around, people shooting guns everywhere. Now, all the shooting that you guys do, the morning Reveille, the loudspeaker announcements, and evening Retreat… All of it just continues to lure them in. Stop making all that damn noise for a few days and we'd get some breathing room."

"You don't get it, do you—I'm sorry, I never got your name."

"Sidney Bannister," she stated, using Lincoln's last name instead of her real name of Wagner. They'd never formalized anything, and had been on the verge of breaking up when he died, but there wouldn't be any records of anything for a long time, if ever, so she'd decided to use his last name. It'd make things easier on the kid.

"Okay, Miss Bannister," he said. "We're out there putting our lives on the line every goddamn day for people like you to cower behind the safety of the walls, while—"

"Sir," Caitlyn interjected.

He turned to her and then gritted his teeth. "You're right, Sergeant. I'm sorry, Sidney. I'm just passionate about this. The men and women up on those walls are the only thing keeping around four million people safe. If we weren't up there killing those things all day and all night, every day, then this place would be overrun in a matter of hours."

"Would it?" Sidney asked. "Think about it logically, not like a soldier."

"*Pfft,*" he spat.

"Okay, that came out wrong," she agreed. "Think about it from a different perspective. Those things are drawn to sight and sound, right?"

"We're pretty sure of it, yeah," he said. "But they could be able to smell too."

"I haven't seen that, and I got myself stuck behind the forward edge of them for more than a month. All I did was observe them—all day, every day," she added for emphasis to let him know that she understood his earlier point. "When they scream, the others with them scream and it alerts others farther away, who scream in response and head toward the original infected who started screaming. And this goes down the line, who knows for how long and how far they echo one another?"

"So they hunt by sight and sound, and we're this giant army base giving off all sorts of noises that travel for miles and miles," the lieutenant said, warming to the idea.

"Exactly."

"Even at night, we're shooting," Caitlyn said, joining the discussion. "We drive the Strykers around and fly helicopters everywhere."

"And those goddamn searchlights," Sidney groaned. "Those are like a visual beacon for probably twenty miles or more."

"Closer to forty out here in the flat desert," Lieutenant Murphy replied. "And then those infected at the forty-mile mark start screaming, bringing in ones from farther out…"

"It's a giant loop of calling them to us," Sidney finished.

"Well, shit," he said, leaning back in his chair. "What are we supposed to do about it?"

Sidney winked at him. "That's when I need you to put your soldier hat back on and figure it out."

"You've given me a lot to think about, Miss Bannister. I don't know what to do with those thoughts yet, but it's definitely an intriguing proposition to *not* be fighting every day."

"I mean, what harm can come from trying to keep quiet and out of sight for one day or one night?" she asked. "Worst case scenario, they build up a giant horde outside the walls and you blast a whole bunch at one time."

He nodded and drank the rest of his water. "Alright. I've gotta go on the wall. I hope to see you again soon, ma'am." He stood and glanced at Caitlyn. "You keep her safe over here, okay, Sergeant?"

"Yes, sir."

They watched the lieutenant leave and then Sidney took a quick bite of the meatlike substance, smiling at Caitlyn. "Damn, girl," the soldier said. "You're good."

"I used to be a lawyer for a non-profit," she laughed. "I got good at convincing people to do what I want by feeding them bits of information and letting them think that they worked things out for themselves."

"Don't try that shit on me."

"Maybe I already have."

11

NEAR LIBERAL, KANSAS
SEPTEMBER 30TH

"There's two of 'em out on the back forty, Mr. Campbell."

The old man sighed and shook his head at the news that John brought. The number of infected had diminished steadily over the last few months, but that didn't mean that he could let his guard down. His family's life depended on him and the boys killing every one of them efficiently, without drawing more to the farm.

"Alright," he exhaled, pushing his half-finished plate of eggs and sausage away from him. "Let's go take care of it."

"Scott and I can take care of it, Mr. Campbell," Jesse, one of the farmhands who'd stayed on, said. "You stay here and finish breakfast. We'll head out and take care of them."

"Thank you for the offer, Jesse, but it don't feel right lettin' others do my work when I'm just as capable of doin' it myself. I was just about done anyways."

"Grandpa, why don't you let Jesse handle this one? You know, stay here at the house in case more come from the west."

He regarded his granddaughter for a moment before speaking. "Now, Katie. I appreciate you trying to keep me safe, but don't you worry about me."

"Grandpa, please. Just let the boys take care of it this time."

Vern glanced over to the ranch hands, Jesse and Scott, and then nodded. They both slugged back their glasses of water, then rushed out of the room.

"There, you girls happy?" he asked his two grandchildren.

"Yes, sir," Sally said, smiling sweetly, her blonde curls bouncing as she nodded. "We think you need to slow down, Grandpa. Maybe even teach us how to help defend the farm one day."

"Now, girls. We aren't gonna go over that again. You're too precious to me. I don't know what I'd do if the same thing that happened to your father happened to either of you."

Vern pulled his plate to him, stabbing a piece of sausage with his fork. He glanced out the window at the pole barn where the ass end of an RV stuck out as a stark reminder of all that the Campbell family had lost. When the outbreak occurred, his son, Jeff and his wife, Katherine, were visiting their daughters at the university up in Lawrence for softball season. They were living the so-called American dream. Both Jeff and his wife retired at forty-five after some lucrative online trading, sold their house and most of their possessions to buy an RV, then spent their time traveling the country. Vern thought it was the dumbest thing his misguided son could have done with his life.

Turns out, the RV was a godsend—in a way. Jeff was attacked and bitten while trying to find the girls on campus. He found them and was able to get them to the RV before he became too weak from blood loss to continue. Katherine drove the RV to the hospital, which was overwhelmed with infected, so they headed straight to Vern's farm. The big vehicle helped them plow through roadblocks that local police and the HiPo set up along Highway 54 in a misguided effort to keep the infection from spreading.

By the time Kat and the girls pulled up, Jeff was too far gone to speak. He turned within an hour of their arrival. They'd locked him inside the RV initially while the girls scoured the Internet for information about the disease and if there was any cure. Of course, there was none. The disease traveled too fast and appeared in too many locations simultaneously for the CDC to do anything about it before they got themselves overrun trying to set up a safe zone in Atlanta.

After a week, Vern made the toughest decision of his life. Even though he and his son weren't as close as he'd have liked it, never in a million years would he have thought he would have to kill his own flesh and blood. By that time, he and the farmhands were already used to dealing with the infected wandering across their land, so it was a simple task to set up a small fence around the door of the RV to let the thing that used to be Jeff out of the vehicle. He'd burst out the door, screaming his hatred like all of them did. He got tangled up in the wire and Vern had to put the emaciated man down with a 9-pound hammer.

Jeff's death, while it sickened him, also gave Vern hope. Upon inspection of the interior of the RV, Jeff had torn the place to shreds. He'd eaten the leather and stuffing from the seats, which told Vern that the infected still needed to eat. Jeff had lost easily twenty pounds in the week he was trapped, even with attempting to eat parts of the RV.

If they could survive long enough to wait them out, the infected would all starve to death.

"Grandpa, can Sally and I go with the boys?" Katie asked.

"What?" he barked, shaking his head to clear away the bad memories. "Didn't I just say no?"

"We need to learn how to defend ourselves, Grandpa," Sally stated. "You and the farmhands have been doing all the work for so long. We both want—no, we *need* to be able to help. With Mom, well, you know. With her the way she is, we need to be able to protect her if the infected make it past the fences."

Kat hadn't been the same since Jeff's death. The two of them were dreamers with their heads in the clouds. They were madly in love, even after more than twenty years of marriage. His daughter-in-law was nearly catatonic for three days after the incident, but eventually came out of it enough to answer simple questions. Even now, months afterward, she usually just sat in the sunroom staring out the windows. A couple of times, she'd made hateful, offhanded remarks about his abilities with a hammer that he mostly ignored. If anything were to make it past the line of defenses that he and the farmhands had devised, then she was a goner for sure.

"They aren't going to make it past the fence," he assured the girls.

"Says you, Grandpa," Katie replied. "You always told us to be self-sufficient and to look after ourselves. Well, so far you and the boys have been doing that for us. What if me and Sally are out one day, without you guys around? It's—"

"Okay, enough," Vern grumbled. They were full-grown women, not the little kids he still imagined them to be. If he was truly trying to protect them and teach them the ways of the world, then they needed to know how to defend themselves against the infected. Maybe it was time. "You're right. I've sheltered you girls long enough. Two of them loonies aren't a major cause for concern, so—"

"Oh, thank you, Grandpa!" Katie exclaimed, rushing over to kiss him on the cheek. Through his younger granddaughter's tangle of dark brown hair, he saw Sally already shrugging into a thick jean jacket, smiling.

Sally high-stepped her way through the tall grass toward the back fields where John had spotted two of the infected struggling against the barbed wire fence. Her hands were slick with sweat on the leather grip of the baseball bat she held. She'd talked about this day for months with her younger sister, Katie. Grandpa finally agreed to let them go out to learn how to kill the infected.

She glanced sidelong at the old man, who'd refused to let the girls go without him. A lifetime spent working cattle, mending fences, and taking care of the farm had kept his body thin and muscular. At sixty-five, he was in better shape than half of the guys back at the University of Kansas where she'd been a sophomore when everything went to hell.

The thought of her friends at the university made her throat tighten, but she didn't have any tears left to cry for them. All of her sorrow had been used up with the death of her father. Those outward signs of weakness were behind her. She had to be strong enough for both Katie and herself, because the Lord knew that her mother was a fruitcake and was no help to anyone.

"So what should we expect up here, Grandpa?" she asked, more to pass the time than having a need to know. She'd cornered Jesse one morning and gleaned as much information as she could from the farmhand.

"Well, sweetheart..." Her grandfather trailed off, likely trying to organize his thoughts. "It's like this. These people, the infected, they aren't really people anymore. They may look like you and me, but whatever they're sick with has destroyed their brains, taking away their humanity. They—"

"So they're zombies then?" Katie asked.

Sally grinned. She and her sister had talked about this distinction at great length. Katie relied on her understanding of popular culture instead of making the mental leap that their reality was something completely different. Sally may have been the blonde, but her brunette sister was much more of a ditz than she was.

"No," Grandpa replied. "They're not zombies."

"How so?" Katie pressed.

"For starters, they don't have to get shot in the head to die. They can be injured just like you and me.

The best we can tell, their brains don't register pain, so it makes it seem like they're indestructible—which they most certainly are not."

"So they're kind of like a druggie high on flakka or something?"

He looked around Sally to Katie. "I don't know what that is, so I can't really compare it. Reminds me of how people on PCP back in the 80s and 90s would act. Your grandmother—God rest her soul—was infatuated with the news after we got cable television out here. She would have it on in the house all day long while she did her housework. When I'd come in at night, she'd give me the condensed version and she thought those dust-heads were one of the signs in the Book of Revelation that the Lord was coming back soon. Shoot, maybe we *are* living in the end days and we are enduring the Tribulation. We just have to keep doing the right thing during these Trials."

Sally groaned inside. Her parents hadn't raised them as Christians, something her grandfather never forgot to mention during his nightly bible reading sessions with them. Since most of what he talked about was completely foreign to the girls, he took it upon himself to teach them the Word of the Lord. The two younger Campbell women entertained the old man, it was only thirty minutes a night, and since there was no television to help pass the time, it didn't really matter that much. The few solar panels that they did have were dedicated to keeping the freezers in the basement working and the well's water pump running.

"So, back to the infected, Grandpa," she said, redirecting the conversation to her original question. "What else should we expect?"

They were less than a quarter of a mile from the furthest field from the house that Grandpa owned. The "back forty" was actually a 65-acre plot that was primarily used for grazing the herd back before a group of infected had decimated it a few months ago. Grandpa had already told them that once they reached the field, they would have to be quiet because the infected had very good hearing.

"You men go ahead," Grandpa told Jesse and Scott. "Make sure the back forty is secure and that we're only dealing with the two that are tangled in the fence."

The two farmhands picked up their pace, each carrying a long metal pole, sharpened to a point on one end. They wore heavy jean jackets, long pants, and heavy gloves. Both of the girls and Grandpa wore the same type of clothing. A smaller metal bar dangled from leather straps hooked through the farmhands' belt loops for close up work and each carried a holstered pistol for the last resort. Non-suppressed firearms were the worst weapons to use against the infected though because it brought any infected within hearing distance screaming toward the sound.

"Let's see," Grandpa continued after the men left. "I already told you girls that they can be killed like any other person, and that they *are not* human, no matter how much they look like it."

"How are you sure that they aren't human?"

Grandpa grunted. "Because humans talk, think, have emotions... These *things* don't do any of that. All they know is death." He paused, waiting to see if either of the girls would ask anything further about the crazies' humanity. When they didn't, he continued. "They are strong—way stronger than a normal person. I've thought a lot about it, I don't think they have any special abilities or any of that Hollywood bull, I just think that their bodies are free to do whatever it can without their brains limiting them. Kind of the same way a hundred and twenty pound mother can lift a car off of her child. That adrenaline rush gives her the strength that she normally wouldn't have."

Sally nodded. She understood the concept. She'd heard stories like that often enough out here in the farming communities when she would stay for the summer with her grandparents. Nothing cool like that happened in Wichita, where her childhood home had been before her parents sold it and bought the RV last year.

She wrinkled her nose when the wind shifted and the smell of rotting meat assaulted her nostrils. "*Ugh*. Is that—?"

"The sickos killed six of my cows before we got out here and took care of them," Grandpa said, pointing toward the gate leading to the back field. "They cornered the poor cows and gouged out their eyeballs… Really tore them up, eating parts of them. *That's* when I truly understood that the infected were beyond the Lord's help. The only thing we can do is put them out of their misery before they infect anyone else."

Grandpa was silent for the last several hundred feet, allowing Sally time to think about their situation and the fact that he'd sheltered the girls from all the killing they'd done over the last several months. Nowadays, they would go several days without an incident, but in the past, they were putting down the infected almost hourly. She'd asked what they did with all the bodies, but he'd always told her that it wasn't her concern.

When they got to the gate leading to the back field, Sally realized that the smell wasn't only from the dead cattle near the fence—those were almost completely rotted away at this point. The smell of death and decay was coming from the *mounds* of dead bodies. Hundreds of them, maybe more.

They'd piled up bodies ten or fifteen feet from the fence line, usually only as tall as the fence itself. Sally thought that was smart, that way the lookout at the house could still see creatures along the fence without the dead blocking their view. She gained a new appreciation for the old man and the three farmhands who'd stayed on to help.

"Oh my God…"

"Don't you take the Lord's name in vain, young lady," Grandpa chastised Katie.

"Sorry, sir."

"Grandpa," Sally said. "Is it safe for all these bodies to remain? I mean, what about disease? Aren't you worried about the diseases from bodies?"

He snorted. "Like what? A virus that could turn us into mindless, feral animals?"

"No, Grandpa," Sally groaned at his attempt at a joke. "I took a freshman history class last semester. And—"

"*Freshman?* You're a sophomore."

"I was a little behind," she replied.

"All that partying with the fraternities. I heard," he said with a disapproving look.

Unbelievable! Sally thought. *Even during the apocalypse, the old Bible thumper finds a way to bring up old shit.* "Anyways..." she drew out the word in annoyance. "My professor said that it was a common tactic in the old days to use catapults to throw dismembered bodies into cities under siege because of the diseases that they carried."

"Plus, it's kind of nasty that you have all these bodies out here," Katie added.

"Jesse figured out that they're attracted by sight," Grandpa said, ignoring Katie's unhelpful statement. "I don't know what a big old cloud of smoke would do. They'd be able to see it for miles around out here on the plains. Might bring more of 'em."

Sally shrugged. "I hadn't thought about that part."

The old man nodded. "We gotta try to think three or four steps ahead, sweetie. Those things won't give us the option to mess up."

"If we can't burn them, could we bury them or something?" she asked.

"Sure. But I don't know that the effort is worth it. We've already got them piled up in the back forty. Every kill that we make on the opposite side of the farm is brought out here to keep away from the house and the rest of the herd. I'm not sure what else we could do."

Sally considered his words as she examined the mounds of bodies. If the infected were attracted to sights, like Grandpa said, then it really didn't make any sense to burn them, as long as nobody from the farm bothered the mounds. Sure, they stunk something awful, but they weren't actively bringing any more of the infected from town out to the farm, so leaving them, as her grandfather suggested, was probably the best option that they had available to them right now.

"So, what should we expect when we get up to that fence line?" she asked, gesturing to Katie as she said it.

"Well, girls, here's the messed up part about the Tribulation—or whatever it is that we're in," Grandpa said. "There will be two—hopefully only two—of the infected tangled up in the barbed wire. Scott and Jesse will make sure that they don't get loose and wait for the two of you to come up. It's going to be your responsibility to put them down."

They walked as Grandpa talked. Ahead, probably only a football field, maybe one-and-a-half football fields, away, Sally could see two people struggling in the wire. From the look of it, the barbs on the fence line were embedded in their skin and what little clothing remained, so she wasn't worried about them getting loose, but the idea of being so close to them freaked her out.

Involuntarily, her hand sought out Katie's and she intertwined her fingers between her younger sister's. "Are you okay?"

"Yeah," Katie replied, hoisting the fireplace poker that she'd brought as her weapon. "I just want to get this over with."

Sally bobbed her chin in agreement. The sooner they'd gotten this *mission* under their belts, the sooner they could begin preparing for tomorrow—and the next day. Because, sooner or later, they wouldn't simply stay on the farm; they were going to have to leave to begin the next stage of their lives.

"Okay, girls. This is gonna sound harsh," Grandpa said as they closed the distance between the fence. "I want each of you to take one of them. Sally, you take the one on the right. Katie, you have the one on the left. I know you both think that I'm an old fool, but I want you to hit them a few times in their bodies, in the arms, the legs if you can reach them. I don't want you to think I'm being mean, now. The lesson here is that they don't feel you hitting them anywhere, so in an emergency, you can't waste your energy hitting them anywhere but the head. Are you girls okay with that?"

They both nodded, neither speaking as they stood only a few feet from their targets. Sally hated herself for thinking of them that way, but if Grandpa was right—and she hadn't seen anything to make her question his tactics—the thrashing and moaning things in front of them were nothing more than a problem to be dealt with.

"Okay. Move on up and hit them a few times in non-vital areas," Grandpa directed.

Sally did as he directed. The thing before her had once been a woman, maybe even the same age as her, but it was clearly emaciated, long months of little or no food had taken their toll on the creature's body. It was nude, except for one shoe, and had an innumerable number of scrapes, cuts, bruises, and even what appeared to be chunks of skin missing from its body. She refused to think of it as a woman, it was simply a threat that had to be dealt with.

What she'd thought of as clothing caught on the fence when she was walking up turned out to be sagging skin snared by the barbs of the fence. Drooping breasts flopped over the wire, the sharpened metal embedded in the soft tissue underneath. Wire dug into flesh, adding to the numerous cuts. It tried to scream, to call others to its location as Grandpa had warned about, but the creature was so dehydrated and parched that only a hoarse, hollow moan came from its throat.

The most unnerving part, Sally thought, was the thing's eyes. It watched her every movement, almost as if it understood what was about to happen, but it couldn't do anything about it. As she stepped closer, those eyes burned into her, consumed by hatred for her. She was alive, uninfected, and the life of the thing in front of her had been taken months ago. It was a shell now, nothing more than a vessel to carry the virus.

Sally swung her bat hard down onto the creature's shoulder. She winced as she felt the clavicle collapse underneath her blow. Just like Grandpa had said, no pain registered on the thing's face. It continued to reach for her, oblivious to the obvious damage to its shoulder.

For some reason, the lack of acknowledgement infuriated her. She'd broken the damn thing's collarbone and it didn't even seem to notice it. She took another downward swing, this one connecting with bone-jarring force along the creature's forearm. A sickening *snap* of bones told her all she needed to know before the hand fell useless, flopping to the side.

Still, the infected didn't register that it had been injured.

"See," Grandpa said. "I told you. They don't feel any pain—watch yourself. It can still get you with its other hand."

Sally grunted in acknowledgement. It was time to put an end to this thing. She set her feet and pulled the bat back over her right shoulder, as if she were in the batter's box, ready to face off against the opposing team's pitcher.

"Careful, now," Grandpa warned. "Make sure you connect cleanly with the head. Otherwise, you'll end up exposing your back. That might not be important right now, with that thing caught on the fence, but it's a good habit to get into and you should strive to keep your movements to a minimum."

"*Okay*, Grandpa," she groaned, swinging hard after she'd said his name. The bat arced from right to left across her body and connected against the temple of the infected in front of her. The bat sank several inches as the skull shattered, driving jagged shards of bone into the brain. It collapsed instantly.

"They still follow our basic human anatomy, so you might have just knocked her out," her grandfather cautioned. "You gotta smash the head in to be sure."

"*Eww!* Do I have to?"

"No. I can do it if you can't."

That set Sally's jaw hard. She could do the same things as the old man. She raised the bat over her head and then brought it down hard on the back of the creature's head. All resistance gave way to complete relaxation when the thing under her bat died completely. It slumped into the fence, dragging the wire downward. A thick, bubbly froth poured from its slack mouth.

The bubbles of gore on the trampled blades of grass mesmerized her. The creature's life was over and she'd been the one to do it. The reality of what she'd done began to sink in, adding to the nausea already rumbling in her stomach from the smells.

"Okay, Katie," Grandpa was saying from nearby. "Just like your sister. One hard hit to the head to end its miserable life."

Sally jumped at the *thud* of her sister's fireplace poker impacting with the head of the infected she dealt with. The sounds of its dying made her dry heave for a moment before its body stopped thrashing.

"Good job, girls," Grandpa praised them as he slid a knife along the throat of each body. Dark red fluid oozed out, mingling with the frothy bubbles on the grass. The blood didn't spurt out in fountains of red mist like the movies, but then she remembered that the creatures were probably already dead from the head injuries. Their hearts weren't pumping blood out of the gash in their necks.

"Now comes the hard part. Jesse, Scott, can you give the girls a hand? I want these corpses off my fence in ten minutes so we can go back to the house and have some iced tea."

The two men grunted in agreement. Sally could tell that they were annoyed at having to escort the girls out there, but Grandpa had insisted on it.

Scott stepped up close to her. "Okay, first, make sure you have your gloves on. You don't want to accidently get stabbed by the wire and get any of their body fluids in it. That happens, and you're a goner."

"Got it," she replied. Just to be safe, she pulled on the cuff of her gloves to make sure they were firmly in place.

"Next, we *always* make sure that they're really dead and not just passed out or something. Your grandfather already took care of that part for us this time, but that's an extremely important part of this job. These things can take a lot of damage—stuff that you and me would be out for the count with—so we usually slit their throats and wait a minute to ensure that they're dead."

The fresh smell of feces stung her nostrils as the muscles in the body in front of her relaxed, adding to the months' worth of dried dung on its legs. Scott wrinkled his nose. "That's actually a good sign," he confirmed.

"After we're sure they're dead—I can't stress that part enough, Miss Sally—we begin untangling 'em. Sometimes they're so tangled up in the wire that we have to cut part of their skin away. It gets pretty gross."

She assisted him as he lifted the body and tried to push it backward. The barbs in the body's chest held it in place, so she had to lift the shrunken, fatty breast tissue up, wiggling the wire until it came free, then the body fell away into the next field.

"Now that it's free," Scott said, "we pull it under the fence and drag it to a pile."

Sally grabbed a hand as he gripped a foot, then they pulled it under the bottom strand of wire. "Let's drag it by the arms," he suggested, wiping his glove on the grass. She didn't want to know what he'd put his hand into.

They each held an arm as they pulled the body behind them. "Why don't we just leave them on the other side of the fence?" she asked.

"A couple of reasons. First, all those bodies would make an easy ramp up and over for the infected. This way, we keep using the fence as it was intended."

"Okay, that makes sense."

"Second," he continued, "Mr. Campbell thinks that they're cannibals."

"Huh?"

"Well, it makes sense. They have to be eating something to stay alive. We've seen them eat grass and you remember the cattle we lost. There have also been a lot of them that we've run across here recently with bite marks and actual chunks missing from their bodies."

"That's just…nasty."

"Yeah, pretty gross, huh?"

They reached the nearest pile and Scott offered to grab the feet while she held the hands. "On the count of three," Scott directed as they swung the body. It landed about halfway up the pile, then rolled back down.

"Sorry."

"It's okay, Miss Sally. That's as good a place as any."

They walked slowly to where Grandpa stood near the center of the field, staring off in the direction of town. "What is it?" Sally asked when they reached him.

"Nothing. I just thought I heard a gunshot from way over yonder."

"A gun? What kinda dummy would be usin' a gun?" Jesse chuckled.

"Now, don't you be making light of someone's misfortune, Jesse," the old man scolded.

"I'm sorry, sir."

Grandpa nodded. "This far along in the game, any survivors know not to use guns unless it's a last-ditch effort."

"You think it was the Cullen brothers, Russ and Tim?" Scott asked.

"No way to tell without going over there," Grandpa said. "And I ain't about to risk our lives by leaving the safety of the farm for those two—especially when every infected in the county will be headed toward the sound of that gun."

"I hope they're alright," Sally remarked. "They used to be so nice to me and Katie when we visited for the summers."

"I don't know," Grandpa rumbled. "I've always gotten a bad feeling from those two. Something about them always seemed a little bit off."

"Oh, you're just mad because they're so much older than us," Katie said, rolling her eyes as they began to walk home.

"You're darned right. What kind of twenty-five year old man hits on fourteen and fifteen year olds?"

"They're harmless, Grandpa," Sally laughed. Of course, she never told anyone, not even Katie, that she'd let Tim play with her breasts when she was sixteen. He'd wanted to go further, but she'd stopped him. Maybe in the back of her mind, she knew that it wasn't right that they were so much older and hanging out with the kids at the city park.

"Harmless, my behind. There's something not right with those two. I can feel it." He smacked his gloved hands on his jeans. "What are the odds that the only other survivors for twenty miles around are those two degenerates?"

Sally laughed quietly at her grandfather's frustration. He was such a wonderful man, but he was going to have to learn to be more trusting of people now that there were so few of them left. *Maybe we should go visit Tim and Russ sometime,* she thought. *I bet they'd like that.*

12

FORT BLISS SOUTHERN WALL, EL PASO, TEXAS
OCTOBER 8TH

It'd been almost a month since Jake had talked to the pregnant woman from the camp. Sidney Ban-something. Their schedules hadn't synched up like they had the morning after the Sam's Club supply run, so he hadn't been able to talk to her again, but he *had* thought about what she said—too much, actually. The infected certainly reacted to sights and sounds, that much was clear.

He glanced at the waning sun and then back across the rubble of the El Paso ruins where the infected in this sector usually filtered through. The light was beginning to change and his men would need to switch to thermals soon. He couldn't see anything moving out there through his scope—but there were several known avenues of approach where line-of-sight was blocked out to about two hundred and fifty meters.

The steady flow of infected had been relatively light the past couple of days, all things considered. That was on top of the reduction over time from those ungodly first few months. Was it time to ask the CO whether they should test Sidney's theory? He'd talked to the Old Man about it a few times and he'd been just as intrigued as Jake had been by the idea. Like the woman had said, what could it hurt besides having a mass of targets below? If their recent activity continued, the hundreds that would trickle in over a few hours' time would be nothing compared to the untold thousands that they'd fought each day and night early on.

Jake walked to the back of his Stryker and looked through the open back door. "Switch to the TWS, Jones," he ordered his gunner inside the vehicle. He watched as the corporal's fingers tapped the Stryker's targeting display to switch from daytime use of the Laser Target Locator Module to the Thermal Weapons Sight and the familiar colors of thermal heat signatures replaced the regular camera view.

Almost immediately, ten or fifteen shapes illuminated. They were behind the scrub brush that grew at six hundred meters, walking steady toward the wall. "Temperature?"

He didn't know why he bothered to ask anymore. There wasn't anyone left within a hundred miles of El Paso that wasn't infected. Everything beyond the walls was already dead, they were just too fucking stupid to know it.

"One-oh-six," Jones replied in his thick Jersey accent. "Permission to engage, sir?"

The fuckers' body temp always spiked when they were active and an uninfected human couldn't survive temperatures like that without being in the hospital. They certainly wouldn't be up walking around.

"Light 'em up."

The large .50 caliber machine gun on top of the Stryker began spitting out rounds at the infected beyond the range of the standard infantryman's ability to engage. Jake watched the display in satisfaction as the figures crumpled under the withering fire. They hadn't tried to take cover or duck out of the way when their buddies began to fall around them, so he knew that he'd made the right call.

The infected were coming out for the night.

All along the base's perimeter, he could hear the heavy machine guns of the other vehicles stationed every fifty feet along the wall. Thinking about those first few months, he was amazed that they'd survived them with only helicopter close air support and dismounted infantry on the single-stacked walls. Over time, the walls had been thickened and heightened and were now two shipping containers tall and two wide in most places, allowing for the Strykers and gun trucks to be driven up on top of the wall to provide heavy weapons support. It added a dimension of depth and firepower to the already considerable stand-off advantage they had. Only the sheer number of infected had been an issue.

Now, that seemed to be changing. *Maybe?*

"Ah, fuck it," he muttered.

"Say again, sir?" Jones asked, turning around in the seat.

"Nothing, man. Just thinking about something else."

"Don't do that to me, sir!" the gunner exclaimed. "I thought maybe you'd changed your mind about me shooting those freaks."

"No, you're okay, Jones. I was just thinking about how there have been less of them than there used to be."

"We've killed everything that ever came this way, sir. Maybe there's just not that many of them left anymore."

Jake thought back to his experience in Midland and shook his head. "Nah, there are *millions* of them left. Maybe even hundreds of millions. Think about it. There are four million here, supposedly fifteen million in New York—and that's it, besides the random people holed up in the middle of nowhere. So, say that's a total of twenty-five million, out of what? Three hundred and eighty million Americans before this all started?"

Jones nodded and then looked at the display screen. He used the joystick to pan the thermals back and forth in his sector to make sure it was clear and then looked back to Jake. "Don't forget about Mexico and Canada, sir."

"Yeah. And South America, and Europe and Asia…"

It was too much. If the higher-ups on post, or whatever was left of the US Government, knew how far-reaching this thing was, then they sure as hell weren't sharing that information with anyone. It made sense, given the relatively slow infection rate for bites and scratches, that someone feasibly could have gotten on a plane and made it to Europe—if it didn't start there in the first place. Jake had no idea what the truth was.

"We're making a dent, though," Jake asserted, unsure if he believed it himself, but knowing that he needed to keep his spirits up in front of the men. "Between us and the Air Force, we've carved out a nice little piece of the desert."

"Hey, sir. Can I talk to you about something?"

"Sure, what is it, Jones?"

"Well..." He trailed off as he tapped on the TWS display to zoom in to an area. Determining that the heat signature posed no threat, he said, "It's only a dog or big cat. Anyways, sir. You know that hot chick that stays with Third Platoon—well, I mean, she would be hot if she wasn't so pregnant. Anyways, you know who I'm talking about?"

Jake grimaced. "Yeah, I've met her." *What the hell is this about,* he wondered.

"Well, she has a theory that pretty much everyone in the Third Herd is on board with. It's crazy as fuck, but it makes sense too, sir."

"Do you mean the one where Able Company gets the entire First Armored Division to cease fire for a couple of days to see if the infected go away?"

Jones nodded. "Yeah, that one, sir. I've been thinking about it a lot. It might just work."

Jake thought about the gunner's background before answering. Jones was smart. He'd graduated from Brown University a little over a year ago with a business degree and more than two hundred thousand dollars in debt. As a result, he joined the Army for the college loan repayment program to wipe out about half of it for a four-year enlistment, pretty good deal—especially now, since being in the Army at Fort Bliss was likely the only thing that kept the kid alive. He was more than just book smart, though, and his ability to see things for how they actually were instead of following the party line had been one of the qualities that Jake admired in him, and often used the enlisted man as a sounding board.

"Yeah. I've been thinking about it a lot too," Jake admitted. "The soldier in me says it's a terrible idea, but when I watch these things' reactions… I don't know. I think it might work."

Jones nodded enthusiastically. "I *know* it would work, sir. We could—*contact!*"

The lieutenant sighed. They wouldn't get an opportunity to test the theory if... "Hold your fire, Jones," he said. "Just hold on. I'm gonna go talk to Sergeant Turner."

"Oh, he ain't gonna like this, sir. Not one bit."

Jake nodded in agreement as he stepped away from the open hatch. The last time he'd seen his platoon sergeant, he was over on the far right flank talking to Sergeant Gallegos. The two of them were only a few years apart in age, which made them by far the oldest in the platoon, so it was natural that they had some type of bond. It turned out that they both loved old MTV shows, the kind that weren't on the air any longer. Well, weren't even on the air when there still was television.

When he walked up, the two old soldiers were arguing over which *Singled Out* co-host was hotter, Jenny McCarthy or Carmen Electra. Turner liked the blonde, Gallegos preferred the brunette. "Hey, Sergeant Turner," Jake interrupted. "Can I get a second?"

"Sure thing, sir. I'm gettin' tired of Gallegos' asinine delusions anyway."

They walked a few feet and the old NCO asked, "What's up, sir?"

Jake took three or four minutes to outline Sidney's idea and his own belief that a cease-fire would work. Once he was finished, he asked, "So what do you think? Is it worth giving it a shot?"

"Sir, can I be candid with you?"

"Of course. I don't—"

"It's the goddamned stupidest idea I've ever fucking heard," Turner bellowed. "Those fucking things don't think. They don't reason. They don't decide that if we go dark and quiet for a little bit that they'll just go away. They are coming after us because they're drawn to us. I don't know how or why—check that, I do know why. They want to spread their virus. We go allowing them to get up close to the walls, they'll eventually find their way to the gates. Once enough of them are pressed up against them, they'll fail, and then they have unrestricted access to all that nice, juicy refugee meat. We allow them to get inside the walls and we risk the extinction of the human race."

Jake chuckled uneasily. "Okay, that's a little dramatic, Sergeant Turner, but point taken. I'm not advocating allowing them inside the walls or even close enough to make us worry about the gates. I just want to see what these things will do if we give them the opportunity to simply go away and die of starvation someplace else."

"I *do* like the idea of them suffering a long, agonizing death alone in the sand," the NCO grunted.

Jake shrugged. "If you need that visual to help you give this a try, then sure." He looked around at the portion of his platoon that he could see. The rest were spread out over a two-mile length of the eastern section of the wall, but those that were nearby seemed to be watching him, waiting for him to give the order. He didn't know how many people that Sidney had talked with, but the fact that Jones knew her was enough to convince him that she talked to a lot of his men.

He focused back on the platoon sergeant before speaking. "I want to give this a try. We're gonna go dark in our sector and I don't want the men to engage any of the infected until I give the order. Understood?"

"You talked to the Old Man about this, sir?"

"No, I haven't discussed it with Captain Massey," he replied.

"Don't you think you should?"

"No," Jake said, shaking his head and using the movement to give him a little more conviction in the plan. "The CO is a man who wants data, evidence that something might or might not work, not just an untried concept. If I can take him some real-world observations about how the infected react, then I might be able to convince him to try it company-, or even battalion-wide."

"Are we really doing this, sir?"

"Yeah, we are. Order the men to hold their fire and don't engage anything—unless it's attacking a refugee trying to make it inside the walls." He flicked a finger at the generators chugging noisily behind them. "We'll cut the generators to turn off the lights. Go dark and keep the men quiet. Then we'll see what happens."

The platoon sergeant stared him in the eyes for a moment and Jake thought he was going to challenge the order. Sergeant Turner dipped his chin slightly and grunted. "I was due a new lieutenant anyways."

Jake frowned as the grizzled NCO went to Gallegos to tell him the order personally. After a few quick sentences and several hurried glances in the direction of the lieutenant, Gallegos nodded and Sergeant Turner walked hurriedly to his Humvee where he picked up the radio and passed Jake's order along to everyone in the platoon.

"Well," Turner called from the front seat. "Looks like your little theory is gonna have a rough first night."

"Why's that?" he asked as he scanned the wreckage in front of his platoon's sector.

"Multiple TWS hits," Turner replied. "Looks like the infected are here for the party."

The NCO's face disappeared in the darkness as someone flipped the switch to turn off the lights, and then cut the motor on the portable spotlight's generator. The action was repeated more or less in order down the line as the pools of light illuminating his men disappeared.

With the generators turned off, Jake could hear the confused screams of the infected as their prey, once visible up high on the wall, disappeared. The creatures continued to advance toward the last place they'd seen humans and Jake prayed that his men could keep calm and not shoot into the crowd of infected that would soon be at their door.

"Here we go…" he muttered under his breath.

13

ABLE COMPANY HEADQUARTERS, FORT BLISS, TEXAS
OCTOBER 9TH

"What the hell were you thinking, Jake?" Captain Massey seethed.

Jake stood at rigid attention in front of his commander's desk. Even though the October temperatures were easily twenty degrees cooler than the heat of summer, beads of sweat ran down his back and pooled along his beltline. Last night hadn't gone like he'd expected it to.

"I—" He stopped and organized his thoughts quickly, leaning on vernacular he'd learned in Ranger School before all of this happened. "Sir, I had a theory that if the unit practiced good noise and light discipline, then the infected would stop their movement toward the base and seek other prey."

"They sure as shit did seek other prey, Lieutenant," a familiar voice boomed behind him as Captain Massey jumped to his feet. Jake shuddered and stared straight ahead at his commander's "I love me" wall of diplomas and certificates. His sleeve rustled as the brigade commander, Colonel Albrecht, pushed past him. "They went after troopers along other sections of the wall."

The colonel turned toward Jake and then sat on the edge of the Able Company commander's desk. "Stand at ease, Lieutenant. Todd," the older man nodded at the captain.

"Good morning, sir," Captain Massey replied as Jake spread his legs shoulder-width apart and clasped his hands behind his back.

"Your theory isn't as hair-brained or potentially as disastrous as what happened on that wall last night, Lieutenant Murphy. Hell, I actually think that something like that might work—if you bothered to communicate to anyone else what you were doing."

Jake pressed his hands into the small of his back, attempting to absorb the sweat there with his uniform. "I accept full responsibility—"

"Can it," the colonel barked. "I don't want to hear about that bullshit—because you're one hundred percent guilty. I just want to know why you didn't talk to your commander, or hell, even the platoons to your left and right on that wall. *They're* the ones that suffered because of this."

Jake frowned. He'd failed his brothers and sisters and people had died because of it. There was no way to sugarcoat the facts. His men had held their fire, allowing the infected to come all the way up to the wall, a lot of them. Then, predictably, they'd turned and continued along the wall, moving toward the units on either side of Able's First Platoon because the other units on the wall were still firing and creating a massive amount of noise. The soldiers in those other units had been focused on the infected out front and never saw the ones piling up from the side until it was too late.

Fourteen soldiers had died before the men and women stationed along the wall were able to close the gap that had opened in the line and burn away the seething mass of infected bodies.

"Sir," Jake said. "I incorrectly assumed that the infected in my sector were wandering back out into the city when we stopped firing and turned off the lights. They just went toward the sound of the gunfire on our left and right."

"Goddamned right they went left and right," Colonel Albrecht stated. "Because you didn't communicate with anyone what you were planning to do. Like I said earlier, Lieutenant, I don't necessarily think your idea is a bad one. If we could get some breathing room, we might be able to have some other options. Dammit, if you would have simply talked to someone else, or picked up the radio and called your battalion so they could have warned the other platoons on the wall that they needed to watch their flanks, this might not have happened. It sure as hell wouldn't have gone down like it did."

Jake nodded his head, but didn't say anything.

"I have fourteen dead troopers because of your actions, Lieutenant Murphy's," the colonel continued, staring hard at Jake. "You're the best platoon leader I have in my brigade, which is why you were chosen to run that proof of concept emergency resupply operation last month. But I can't let last night's leadership failure go unpunished." He paused and then asked, "What's your recommendation, Captain Massey?"

Jake's ears perked up. He knew there'd be some type of punishment, but he couldn't imagine what it could be. The Army thrived on good order and discipline—part of that was making people feel it in their pocketbook or by restricting them to base, neither of which applied anymore since the soldiers weren't being paid and there was nowhere to go.

"Sir, I recommend confinement for a week."

The colonel glanced sidelong at Todd Massey and crossed his arms over his chest. "Confinement? Where the fuck are we going to confine him? All of us are already confined."

Massey nodded as the colonel tapped his chin with a finger. "I could shoot you. General Bhagat would support my decision." Jake blanched. The older man's affable demeanor belied what was truly going on in his head. "Your actions directly resulted in the deaths of American soldiers—of human *survivors*."

"Sir, if I may?" Jake recognized the brigade sergeant major's voice coming from beside him, but he didn't dare to look away from the colonel.

"Go ahead, Sergeant Major."

"Sir, I agree with you that the lieutenant's actions were irresponsible, poorly coordinated, and potentially disastrous for the entire base if those infected would have gotten past the soldiers on that wall. He fucked up—big time. But maybe he doesn't truly understand what we're doing here, who we're protecting—hell, I'm not sure if any of us do."

The sergeant major stepped closer to the colonel and into Jake's peripheral vision. He was a tall, thin black man with graying hair. "You know I grew up in a tiny little Mississippi town, sir. We didn't have jack shit in our town, everyone was poor as dirt and times were hard. Every two years, political candidates would roll through the county seat a few towns over and tell everyone that they were going to make things better, that they understood our problems. Well, I tell you what, things never got better because those politicians didn't truly understand what we were going through, so they *couldn't* fix it."

"Okay. So what's your recommendation?" Colonel Albrecht asked.

"The lieutenant, and all of us soldiers over here getting hot food, sleeping in beds with mattresses and air conditioning—we're like those politicians. We think we know what's best for all of those refugees over there, but we don't know shit about what's happening *inside* the camps. We keep them pinned up, escort aid workers and food trucks, but we don't know how they feel, what their fears are, or understand their hopes that their families will be safe. I think the lieutenant should be confined in the refugee camp. It'll give him an opportunity to learn to truly empathize with the refugees, teach him what he's fighting for, and most importantly, what we stand to lose if he goes off on some half-assed, hair-brained operation without telling anyone about it."

The colonel grimaced. "That's good advice, Sergeant Major. It's a direction that I hadn't even considered going." He stood and walked around the office for a moment, appearing to be deep in thought, and then he finally turned back. "Alright. I like it. Have legal draw up the paperwork. I want to sign it by the end of the day. Lieutenant Murphy, at 0800 tomorrow morning, you'll be escorted, in civilian clothes, to the refugee camp in the Ready First sector. You'll be confined within the camp, living amongst the refugee population for four weeks as punishment for your inability to effectively communicate your plan, which ultimately ended up getting fourteen soldiers killed."

The older man sat on the edge of the desk and re-folded his arms. "Any questions, Lieutenant Murphy?"

Jake's mind churned as he tried to think of what he should ask. Four weeks seemed like an incredibly long time. *Tell that to those men who died*, he chided himself. *They'd love to have those weeks back.*

"No, sir. I don't have any questions," he replied, feeling terrible for what happened.

"Good. And smart," Colonel Albrecht said. "If you'd have argued, I would have made it longer. Now get out of here and go pack your things."

Jake snapped to the position of attention and saluted. Colonel Albrecht stared hard at him for a moment and then returned the salute as if he were annoyed. Jake spun on his heel and made his way out of the room quickly.

Once he was in the orderly room, he maneuvered around the cots set up for the overnight radio watch guys and stepped outside. He stumbled a little as he descended the steps down to the sidewalk below.

He'd walked for forty feet before he realized that his room was in the building he'd just left. "Fuck it," he grumbled and continued along the sidewalk until he was in the shadow of the adjacent building. There was a vacant picnic table there, so he sat and rested his head in his hands.

"What the fuck?" he moaned. "What the fuck did I do?"

His orders had gotten those men killed. He could have simply had his men carry on as always, killing the ever-present infected, and then they would still be alive. It was his fault for not getting permission from Captain Massey to go ahead with the idea. Massey would have run it up the flag pole and there could have been a coordinated effort to try it one evening.

He felt the presence of someone standing in front of him before he noticed the shadow on the ground. "Everything okay, Lieutenant?"

He used his palms to scrub at the corners of his eyes. When he looked up, he was surprised to see Sidney, the woman who'd planted the seed about the cease fire in his mind. For a brief moment, he wanted to blame *her* for what happened. If she hadn't said anything, then he wouldn't have decided to try to not defend the wall. It was her fault, wasn't it?

No. It's not her fault, he thought. *The fault lies with me. I didn't do things the right way. I wanted to be the hero that figured out how to stop the attacks, so I didn't let anyone know what we were doing. It's not that woman's fault. Accept your punishment and move on.*

"Uh... Yeah. I'm good," he lied.

"Mind if I sit?"

He sat up and placed his back against the table, gesturing toward the seat. She sat down beside him, legs facing outward as his were. "I heard about last night."

He grunted. "How the hell did you hear about it?"

She pointed at the opposite building, painted desert tan like all of the others surrounding it. "I live right there with a squad leader from Third Platoon and one of your squad leaders. Something like this isn't going to stay quiet."

He sighed. "Yeah. I guess not."

"It didn't quite go like I thought it would," she stated. "I'm sorry."

"It's not your fault," Jake countered. "You're a civilian and you had an idea. I'm the officer. I acted on your idea. But the reason it didn't work is because I failed to tell the adjacent units what I was doing, so they didn't stop firing their weapons, and that brought the infected to them." He cursed and spat into the dirt. "If I'd told them what we were doing, they could have either watched their sides where they thought we were protecting them, or they would have given the theory a shot as well. The blame lies with me, not with you."

She was quiet, so he looked over at her. She leaned back against the table as well, her fingers absently trailing along her protruding stomach. "Are *you* okay?" he finally asked.

"*Mmm hmm*," she said. "Just thinking." She stopped rubbing her belly and looked at him. "So are they going to punish you or something? That's the rumor going around the fourth floor."

"*Hmpf*, figures," Jake grunted. "Yeah, I'm getting a punishment. Since we aren't being paid, and we're already confined to base, the traditional Army punishments won't work. So, the commander sentenced me to a month in the refugee camp. Isn't that fucked up?"

Her nostrils flared. "You mean fucked up that you have to go down there or fucked up that he views that as a punishment?"

"The latter," Jake stated, sensing her anger.

She seemed to relax slightly. "Look, Lieutenant, I—"

"You can call me Jake. Hell, for the next four weeks, I'm not even going to be a lieutenant, just another refugee," he added bitterly.

Sidney nodded. "Jake. I like that. Much more approachable than Lieutenant Murphy." She paused and then continued rubbing her stomach. "What I was going to say is that it's not going to be that bad for you down in the camps. At least you know that it's only temporary and you have a way out. Everyone else down there? Not so much."

"Yeah," he agreed. "But do I have a way out? Do *we* have a way out? I'm starting to think this whole thing is just delaying the inevitable."

Sidney's lips thinned. "I've thought the same thing—a lot, actually. I'm not normally a defeatist, but there are too many people in here. Too many infected out there."

Jake sighed. "You're right. There was an incredible amount of food brought here over the weeks leading up to when we closed everything down, plus everything the FEMA camps had around the city. But even all of that isn't enough; we're running out. There were never supposed to be four million people behind those walls. Planners thought there would be one million inside and the rest would be in the camps outside the walls for a couple of months at most. We were supposed to have the threat taken care of by now."

"There's probably three hundred million people infected in this country alone, Jake. And the virus seems to make the infected seek out new hosts. That means we're the only game in town. And that means they're not going to stop coming."

He turned to stare at her. "So what are you saying?"

"Sooner or later this place is going to fall—whether it's from the infected getting in, someone getting bitten while they're on duty on the wall and turning once they're inside the base, or more likely, we'll run out of food and those four million people will destroy everything."

"What can we do about it?" he asked, his alarm growing because she voiced some of the same concerns that he had.

"Nothing. Fort Bliss is a sinking ship. Once this baby is born and given a clean bill of health, I'm leaving."

He blanched. "You can't. You haven't been out there since—"

"I'll be fine. I was out there for months before coming here and I almost didn't come inside the walls." She held up her hands. "Don't get me wrong, I'm grateful for the protection that I've gotten and the food that I've been given, but… You'll see when you go down to a camp. This place is a powder keg and it's ready to explode."

Sidney pushed herself up in that odd, characteristically pregnant way, rolling sideways onto one hip and then arching her back to lift her butt off the bench. "I'm gonna go inside and try to get a little bit of sleep before the shift change and all the soldiers come into the barracks," she said.

"Alright, see ya later," he replied. She waved and began to walk toward the barracks.

"*Hey!*" Jake called after her.

She turned. "Yeah?"

"Any advice for the camps? I mean, like any idea what I should do to fit in?"

"Yeah. Don't tell anyone that you're a soldier and don't tell them that you're there as punishment for a few weeks. That will make this whole place implode."

She turned back and continued toward her room.

"*Hmpf,*" he grunted. To be honest, he hadn't thought about it from the refugees' perspective. He was planning on being honest when anyone asked, now he was reconsidering. That little riot last month wouldn't even compare to what would happen if all the refugees rose up at the same time over the perception of inequity between them and the soldiers.

He'd have to be careful not to start another massive uprising, which was a lot for Colonel Albrecht to put on his shoulders. He was only a lieutenant and hadn't been given any warnings about the consequences... The realization hit him hard.

"Holy fuck," Jake muttered, remembering the day he was in the division commander's office with Colonel Albrecht after the Sam's Club run. The general said the death of twenty thousand refugees was a godsend. He'd spoken in such a cold, detached manner that Jake had wondered if he'd thought of the refugees as people at all. Was there a plan in place all along to send someone to the camps as punishment to get the refugees riled up? If the Army were to put down a major riot, thousands upon thousands of people could be killed—which meant fewer mouths to feed. *Am I being paranoid or is that why he's sending me to the camps?*

There was no way he'd know for certain if the colonel and the division commander had devised an elaborate plan to kill off a lot of the civilians without getting the blame, but it made sense in a sick and twisted way. Less people to feed meant that humanity could survive longer, maybe long enough to kill off the infected as winter set in and millions of them died from exposure.

"Son of a bitch," he grumbled. "I hate being a pawn."

14

ABLE COMPANY HEADQUARTERS, FORT BLISS, TEXAS
OCTOBER 10TH

"You have everything you need in that bag?" Captain Massey asked Jake skeptically as he examined the medium-sized, black backpack that he wore.

"The government will provide everything I don't have," Jake replied.

"What do you mean?"

"If I'm going to be treated like a refugee, then I'm going to act the part, sir."

"Is this a game to you, Lieutenant?"

"No, sir. I have my 9-millimeter, a knife, a blanket, a few changes of clothes, my hygiene kit, an extra pair of tennis shoes, and a few cans of food. That's all that a new refugee coming onto Fort Bliss would have—maybe a little more, but I don't want people thinking I'm a soldier and that we punish soldiers by forcing them to live in the same conditions that the refugees live in."

The commander glanced at the orderly room NCO and the company's other three lieutenants, who were here to see Jake off. Joe and Brian were his roommates, so it wasn't a surprise that they were here, but Grady making his way from his quarters was a nice gesture. "Sergeant, can you give us a moment?" Massey asked the NCO.

"Yes, sir." The soldier slipped out the front door and stood on the concrete stoop outside.

Once the door was shut, Captain Massey turned back to Jake. "What's going on, Jake? Don't make a fucking scene. Just do your time and come back to your platoon."

"I'm not making a scene, sir. But I do feel like I'm being used as bait."

"What the hell are you talking about? You received an extremely lenient punishment for getting fourteen men killed because of your stupidity."

"Just let it go, man" the company executive officer said. Jake had told Joe and Brian about his belief that the division commander was trying to reduce the refugee population and both of them thought he was crazy.

Jake shook his head. "No. I've given this a lot of thought. It's the only thing that makes any goddamned sense."

"Which is?" the captain asked.

"Sir, I think the division and base leadership want the number of refugees reduced. It's simply not sustainable from a logistics perspective."

"You're right, it's not," the commander agreed. "But what does *you* receiving non-judicial punishment have to do with our unsustainable installation population problem?"

He took a few minutes to explain his theory, and all the while, the captain's face remained blank. Until he finished, then it changed into a look of sadness, or pity, Jake wasn't sure which. "Jake, this is all going on in your head. Just like the idea to not kill the infected the other night, it's simply not the reality that we live in. The division commander isn't trying to secretly stage a revolt to kill off the refugee population. Do we need you to see the psych before you carry out your punishment?"

"What?" Jake choked on the saliva in his mouth. "No, sir. I'm good to go. I just—" In his periphery, Joe shook his head. "Never mind, sir. It's just a theory that I don't have any proof for. And no, I don't need to see a shrink. I'll do my time down in the camp, then come back up here and do my job."

The captain stared at him for a moment, assessing whether he told the truth. Finally, he nodded and said, "Alright. Head down to the motor pool. Sergeant Gallegos has a Humvee waiting to take you to Refugee Camp Number Three."

"The one where there was already a riot?" Jake asked in disbelief.

"It's the one we have in the brigade sector. We can't keep you safe if you aren't in our area of operations."

"Yeah..." He trailed off. The uncertainty he'd experienced over whether his fears were real or not had vanished. They were sending him into a camp that had already experienced unrest and a lot of people had died, which automatically created more enemies. He'd learned about insurgencies when he was a cadet at West Point. One of the reasons kinetic counterinsurgency fights almost always failed in the long run was because killing, beating, and arresting insurgents almost always created more enemies in their friends and family. *That's* what he was walking into at Camp Three. Twenty thousand dead out of a population of close to four hundred thousand.

The commander wanted them to revolt. Four hundred thousand people ate a lot of food.

"I don't wanna get up," Sidney murmured into the soft flesh of Caitlyn's arm. She was comfortable, and warm, with her face buried in the crook of the soldier's arm as the woman spooned her from behind.

"I know, but I gotta go to work. So do you."

"*Ugh*," she groaned. It was getting harder these days to wake up, even though she knew that her job in the kitchen was one of the only things keeping her out of the camps. The other was Caitlyn, but she was just a staff sergeant and didn't have the authority to house and feed a refugee in the barracks.

She wriggled her body forward, reluctantly breaking contact with her friend and the warmth she radiated. It took her a moment to make it off the bed, while behind her, she felt the pressure on the mattress springs release as Caitlyn rolled off the bed to the floor.

Sidney arched her back, standing fully. Gallegos was already gone. "When did Luis leave?"

"*Mmm*, about two hours ago; maybe only an hour and a half. He had to escort Lieutenant Murphy down to Refugee Camp Three before his platoon's shift on the wall. Poor bastard has to have the XO as a platoon leader until Murphy gets back."

"XO?"

"The company executive officer, the number two guy. He was the MGS Platoon leader before Lieutenant Hallewell got here. He's an asshole."

"Oh, that sucks."

"Yeah, well, good for me at least. Since Gallegos is undoubtedly going to be at work for a lot longer than normal, I'm gonna move to the top bunk while he's on shift to give you the entire bottom bunk. I love ya like a sis, Sidney, but I need more room."

"Of course," she replied. "I don't want to be a burden."

"You're not. *Buuut*," Caitlyn drew out the word. "You think you could be gone tonight from like eighteen hundred to twenty hundred?"

"I think I can find something to do."

"Good. Mamma needs a little alone time with Dickerson. He's hung like a horse—well, you know, you've seen him in the shower."

Sidney laughed. "I hadn't really noticed."

Caitlyn shimmied her camouflaged pants over her hips, sending her ample breasts swaying side to side. "Come on! You're telling me that with all those hormones raging inside of you, you aren't horny as hell? I couldn't stop fucking when I was pregnant with Jocelynn—"

The sergeant stopped suddenly and turned away. "I'm sorry," Sidney offered, unsure of what else to say.

Caitlyn nodded and took a ragged breath. "It's okay. It's been a long time. Isn't that what they say, that all wounds heal with time?"

"Yeah, I guess so."

Her friend pulled a pink sports bra over her head, followed quickly by the olive green undershirt. "Okay, I'm gonna go brush my teeth and put my hair up. You coming?"

"I need a minute to stretch," Sidney replied. "My back is killing me."

"It's these mattresses. They suck."

Sidney grunted a response, to which Caitlyn said, "Alright, I'll see you down there."

"Well, hell," Sidney said aloud once the soldier was gone. She'd been making moves toward Dickerson, hoping the young soldier would want to hook up so she could relieve *her* sexual tension. She'd lied to Caitlyn, but she sure as hell needed a release as well—and the idea of having a potential protector was part of her singling him out.

Sidney glanced at the frameless mirror glued to the barracks room wall and lifted her shirt to reveal her swollen stomach. She was seven months along. She had two more to go, then maybe two or three more after that and she was leaving Fort Bliss. Preferably not alone. It was a scary world out there, especially for someone with an infant, and that giant of a man, Dickerson, would have been a good companion, even if he was a little dense.

She sighed again and dropped her shirt as she mussed up her hair. It was longer on the top than she used to keep it, but still cut short on the sides. The scene from *Silence of the Lambs* where Buffalo Bill uttered his famous line, "I'd fuck me," crept into her mind, making her laugh a little bit.

An hour later, Sidney was at the kitchen, pouring powdered milk into giant mixing bowls to reconstitute it. It was mind-numbing work, menial in every way, but at least it kept her out of the camps and allowed her to have some type of purpose. Life in the camps was measured by the time between meals and little else mattered.

Throughout her shift, she thought about the problems with the base and its inevitable fall. Surely the base leadership knew that they couldn't feed everyone forever. What was their plan for the long run? Just as she'd spoken to Lieutenant Murphy yesterday, there was no end in sight to the siege.

It all came to her at once. Jake was being used, why else would they send him down there? Before her talk last night, he'd probably planned on wearing his uniform and simply doing his time without trying to hide the fact that he was a soldier being punished. They *wanted* more riots. Short of kicking people out or allowing an entire camp to become infected, it was the only way to get rid of a large number of people.

"Lieutenant Murphy…"

"What?" Helen, her shift supervisor, asked from where she poured thirty-pound bags of flour into large vats to make bread.

"I— I need to go, Helen."

"What for? We've still got two hours left for breakfast and then we have to start lunch."

Sidney clutched at her stomach. "I need to go see the doctor. I think something may be wrong with the baby."

Helen's eyes shot upward. "Oh my goodness! Do you need me to drive you to the hospital?"

Sidney hated lying to the woman. She'd been extremely nice to her since she arrived and was lenient on tardiness as long as all of the work got done. "No, thank you. I have my roommate's Jeep."

"Are you sure?"

Sidney nodded, untying the apron she wore. "Yeah. I know I'm overreacting, but I just think it's better if I go get checked. It's probably gas, no big deal."

"Okay... You go ahead and take the rest of the day off, sweetie. We'll be fine."

"Are you sure?"

"Of course. Go get yourself checked out and then go get some rest."

Sidney hugged Helen's shoulders. "Thank you. I really could use a nap."

"Go on, then," Helen grunted. "We've gotta get these biscuits made for the second breakfast shift."

Sidney left, hunching over slightly to play up the alleged pain in her stomach. The baby inside her kicked in response to his space being imposed upon. "Oh, stop it," she chastised, straightening once she was out the back door.

She had to warn Jake about why she thought they decided to punish him by sending him into the refugee camp. Gone was her indignation that the military viewed the refugees' predicament as a prison. Now she was furious that they were probably planning outright murder.

She couldn't remember if Gallegos was at the company or at the motor pool to escort Jake to the camp. The company was on the way to the motor pool from where she was now, so that's where she would stop first.

"Can I help you, ma'am?" the NCO in the orderly room asked when she stepped inside.

"I'm looking for Lieutenant Murphy," she blurted. "I have important news to tell him."

"Ma'am, he's—"

"I've got it, Sergeant Demers," someone called from the office in the back corner.

Sidney looked up expectantly, noticing the light blue plaque by the door read "**Company Commander**". A short man with close-cropped brown hair came out of the office, angling directly for her.

"Ma'am, Lieutenant Murphy is on a mission," the man, wearing captain's bars stated. "He'll be gone for about a month. Is there something I can do to help you?"

"He's not on a goddamned mission," Sidney replied. "He's been sent down to the refugee camps for punishment."

His expression hardened slightly. "That's correct. Who are you?" His eyes roved up and down her body quickly. "Are you his girlfriend?"

"What? No. I'm a friend. He's in danger. They're sending him down to the camp to get the refugees riled up again so they can—"

"Oh not this shit again," the officer groaned. "He's been gone for two hours, ma'am. You'll have to wait until his time is up at Camp Three."

"Camp Three?" Sidney repeated. Any doubt she'd harbored that the military was setting up a mass extermination of refugees evaporated. Refugee Camp Three was a powder keg, ready to explode. The only reason they'd send Jake to that camp was to light the fuse.

"Yeah. Camp Three. That's the only camp in First Brigade's AO—ah, area of operations. Jake had the same reaction this morning." A look of concern passed across the captain's face. "He was concerned with the camp being a flashpoint for riots too."

"Look, uh, Captain Massey. I work in the First Brigade dining facility and we're constantly making things with less than half of the ingredients—and that's for the soldiers protecting this place. There are four million refugees inside these walls and no way to rapidly replenish the food supply once it's gone. The base leadership knows that."

"Why are you here?" he sighed.

"I figured it out this morning and I'm trying to warn him to blend in—more than I already have."

"You didn't figure this out until just now?" he asked, eliciting a nod from Sidney. "He already figured it out, then. He told me what he thought General Bhagat and Colonel Albrecht are trying to do."

"He did?"

"Yeah. I don't have the authority to overrule the brigade commander, so he was taken to the camp this morning."

"Son of a bitch."

The captain raised an eyebrow, but wisely kept his mouth shut.

"You might have just signed the death warrant on millions of people," Sidney accused, stifling a sob.

She turned and rushed as quickly away from Able Company as she could.

15

SURVIVOR CAMP #3, EL PASO, TEXAS
OCTOBER 12TH

"Get out of here!" a fat man grumbled. How he'd managed to remain so obese for more than six months of reduced rations was beyond Jake. "Ain't no empty bunks and ain't no extra floor space."

The lieutenant waved. "Sorry, folks. I was just trying to find a permanent place to lay my head."

That seemed to be the wrong thing to say. "Why's that?" the fat man asked, sitting up straighter on his bunk. Jake noticed the man held the upper receiver of a disassembled AR-15 and must have been cleaning it. Several other men eyed him suspiciously.

Their weapons were fully assembled and looked ready to rock.

"I just traveled down from the DFW. I tried to hold out on my own, but I ran out of food, so I made the decision to come to El Paso where the Internet said this refugee survival camp was. Of course, that was before it went out a few months ago. Back then, all those FEMA camps still existed. I didn't know things were so shitty here or else I'd have just stayed out there." He threw his head in the direction of the walls.

The man grunted and hunched back down. "Try over in Section ZB. That area that got hit hard when them fuckin' soldiers murdered everyone. They may have some space on the floor."

Jake nodded his thanks and backed out of the tent, allowing the flap to trail across his shoulder as he left, not wanting to turn his back on the crowd inside. These men were not people to be trusted, but they had given him a good idea to try the area that had seen a drop in population recently. What could it hurt?

He'd spent the last two days and nights on the move, finally settling against the side of a tent on the first night and then up against the cold metal of the wall last night. The mood in the camp was entirely transparent. They were unhappy with the status quo and were ready to do something about it. Without even trying to eavesdrop, he'd heard multiple people talking about the lack of proper nutrition and that the soldiers were fed better than they were. This place was ready to explode and placing him here made it seem like that was exactly what the general wanted.

He ducked his head, keeping his face relatively hidden as he passed a squad of soldiers patrolling the muddy walkway between the camp sections. That's all he needed was to be spotted and recognized. At least when he'd been dropped off, Sergeant Gallegos had gone through the motions of pretending to tell him where things were in the camps so he wasn't outed right away.

When the group passed, he lifted his head and trudged through the mud. Every sucking step splatted the brown fluid onto his pants legs and coated the waterproof boots he wore, sending a foul odor into the air. What made it even more disgusting was Jake's knowledge that it hadn't rained in over a week. He was walking through runoff from the latrines.

Sector ZB was near one of the many burn pits. The pits were really just a series of side-by-side large metal dumpsters that sent their foul black smoke into the air almost constantly as members of the Civilian Division poured diesel fuel into the various containers to burn whatever was on the menu. The sweet, yet acrid, smell on the air told him they were burning shit right now. Given the size of the flames, he guessed they were burning at least a week's worth of it.

"*Ugh*," Jake said, pulling his t-shirt up over his nose and mouth.

"You'll get used to it soon enough, *Jake*," a voice said from nearby.

He spun, allowing the fabric over his mouth to drop slightly. A petite Latina woman sat on a folding camp chair beside the entrance to a sleeping tent. "Carmen?" he coughed.

She stood and sauntered toward him, but then stopped and turned quickly. He watched in confusion as she grabbed her camp chair, collapsing it and putting it on her shoulder, before turning back to him. She walked to where he stood in the path.

"What are you doing here, *Lieutenant*? And why are you in civilian clothes, growing a beard," she asked, reaching out to scratch at his stubble.

He pulled his head back in annoyance. Carmen was the woman they'd found inside the Sam's Club in Midland. He hadn't been able to keep his promise to her about keeping her and her kids out of the refugee camp and she'd been pissed. Now, fate had brought them back together and she was probably going to expose him as an Army officer to the hundreds of people milling around.

Jake attempted to change the direction of the conversation. "Why'd you pick up your chair?"

"Because everything gets stolen here," she hissed. "Someone even stole my baby's teddy bear. Can you believe that?"

"I—"

"Of course you can. But you don't care, do you?"

"I—"

"Big, bad Officer Jake. Steals people's food supplies. Forces them to leave their homes. Breaks his promises. You don't—"

He clamped a hand over her mouth and pressed his opposite hand against the back of her head to bring her close. She squealed in fright and wriggled to get away from him. "Would you shut up?" he hissed, looking around wildly to see what the other refugees would do.

Some watched disinterestedly, while others turned away. Nobody offered the woman assistance. They'd likely seen women assaulted hundreds of times since their internment at the camp began. Their indifference struck him as if he'd been punched. These people had no hope.

"I need you to be quiet," he said. "Can you do that?"

She nodded and he eased the pressure of his hand, keeping it in place if she tried to continue her tirade against him.

"Fine," she grunted. He cautiously moved is hands away. "What are you doing here?"

"We've gotten reports that another riot is imminent," he lied, thinking quickly on his feet. "I was sent in here to determine the threat level to the other refugees and to the base personnel. If morale is as bad as the informant said it is, then we may have a major problem and a lot of people could get hurt."

She eyed him suspiciously. "I don't know a lot about the Army, but it seems strange that they'd send an officer—a combat guy like you—to do that. Why not send an intelligence agent or whatever?"

"Well, we don't really have a huge pool of soldiers to choose from," he whispered. "We only have what was on the base before the gates were sealed. There are only so many people that the command thought could pull this off and all of us got tapped. There are soldiers going to the other camps as well. If the population riots and the Army has to put it down, then it could mean the end of humanity."

Her eyes widened in response to his statement—which wasn't false, *per se*. "I hadn't thought about it like that before."

Jake nodded seriously. "It's not a good situation." He gestured around them. "Obviously. But our survival as a species is more important than the survival of a few individuals and troublemakers."

"Wow..." she laughed. "For a second, I almost believed you."

"What?" he asked. "I'm telling you the truth."

"You know, maybe if you hadn't already lied to me and convinced me that life would be better at Fort Bliss—oh yeah, and that you'd keep me and my kids out of the refugee camp—then maybe I'd be gullible enough to believe you."

"Now wait a goddamned minute, Carmen. I tried to get you and your kids housing." He stopped, suddenly aware that he'd spoken loudly. He dropped his voice. "They wouldn't put you up anywhere, every place that can take a family is full."

She spat onto the ground. "This place is shit. My kids have to fight for food scraps and get beat up by the larger ones. I'm constantly defending myself against rape. Women are taken in the night and never heard from again."

Jake glanced at the refugees milling nearby indifferently. "I'm sorry."

She unslung the folding chair from her shoulder and thrust it at him, causing him to throw up both hands to block the assault. "I even have to carry my chair around with me or it will get stolen, *pendejo*."

"I— Really? What the fuck?"

"You're telling me what the fuck? I should be asking you what the fuck, Jake? You were supposed to protect us. We should have stayed at that warehouse. We had enough food, medicine, and supplies to last for decades, maybe even our entire lives. Here, we're just waiting to die."

Her words stung deeper than they should have. He barely knew the woman. In all honesty, he *didn't* know the woman. He knew her name and that she had two kids, that was about it. He shouldn't have been bothered by what she said. He'd known life in the camps was tough.

"Look, Carmen. I'm gonna level with you, okay?"

Her eyes narrowed. "Why would I believe anything *you* say?"

He looked around again. Nobody seemed to care at all about the two people standing near the shit canal. "I'm not here to assess the volatility of the situation in the camps—but I do believe that's why they sent me."

"What do you mean? How can you be here not to do something if that's why they sent you? You talk out of both sides of your mouth."

"No. Hear me out," he pleaded. "I need an ally in the camps."

"Well, you're barking up the wrong tree."

"Dammit. I'm sorry about the warehouse. I had my orders to clear the place out. In fact, I had the authorization to neutralize anyone who we happened to find there if they weren't willing to let me take the food."

"Neutralize?"

"Yeah. I was ordered to get that food by any means necessary. Understand the stakes now?"

She nodded, but didn't answer, so Jake took that as his cue to continue talking. "Like I said, I need an ally here and I'm *not* here to spy. I got sent here for one month as a punishment."

"*Ha!*" she barked. "Oh, that is good. They send you down here when you get—"

He closed the distance and clamped his hand over her mouth again. "Shut it. This is real life or death stuff—not just for me, but for all of humanity. I was telling the truth about that."

"*Mmpfmpfmm.*" He released her and she asked, "What are you talking about now?"

"You weren't here yet, but about a month ago, there was a big food riot and twenty thousand people were killed."

"They were still burning bodies and cleaning the blood when we came to the camp," she stated.

"That's right. We were gone when it happened and you were brought here right afterwards."

"*Pendejo,*" she repeated her earlier insult.

"I was at Division when—" He stopped, noting the confusion on her face. "That's the headquarters building for the Army here on Fort Bliss. The guy who runs this entire operation works there. Anyway, I was up there meeting with the general and learned about the massacre. As I was leaving, I heard him tell my commander that he wished more people would get killed off so the food supplies we have would last longer."

"*Dios mío...*"

"Yeah. With four million people, the food goes quickly and it's beginning to run out—or at least they are planning for when it runs out. That's why we've been raiding the FEMA camps, grocery stores, and food distribution centers within helicopter range."

"And an instant fix would be less mouths to feed," Carmen finished his thoughts.

"Exactly. If there were more riots and more deaths, less people would need food and it would last longer."

"There were *children* who died. Mothers. Fathers. This is evil."

Jake nodded and checked their surroundings once again to see if anyone was listening. As before, nobody seemed to care. "I agree with you, but I can also see where the general is coming from. He's been tasked with keeping *humanity* alive, not every human."

"That's a terrible thing to say," she said, her eyes drifting toward the ground.

"I know. I know it is."

After a moment, she looked up at him, wiping away a tear with the back of her hand. "I should have never brought my babies to this place."

Jake wasn't sure what to do, but hugging her seemed like the right thing. He slowly brought his hands up, leaning in and stopped when he felt the pressure of something pointed sticking into his gut.

He looked down to see the tip of Carmen's knife digging into his shirt.

"Get off me."

"Yup. You're right. Sorry," he said, backing up.

"So that doesn't tell me why you're here. Are you supposed to *start* this fight?"

"What? No!" he exhaled forcefully. "I'm here because I got some people killed. We know the infected are drawn toward sound and movement and all of our actions on this base, on the wall, continue to bring more and more of them. So, I had the idea that if we just stopped shooting them they'd go away and give us some breathing room."

"Did it work?"

"It did for my men, but the infected followed the sounds to the next platoon on the wall that was still fighting. They didn't know we weren't protecting their backs and the infected were able to get to the soldiers on the wall. I'm here as a temporary punishment for letting them get killed."

She stared blankly at him for a moment, making him wonder if she was working through what he said or if her mind had drifted. Finally, she reached out and grabbed his hand, tugging him toward the tent she'd been sitting in front of when he arrived.

"Come on. We've got to get you out of the open and get you some dirty clothes."

He let her lead him along. "Does that mean you'll help me blend in for the next month?"

"Yes. But that also means you're going to help me leave this deathtrap."

"I can't get you billeting outside of the camp."

"I know. If I help you, you're going to take me off of Fort Bliss. I'll find somewhere to live with my kids outside these walls."

For the first time in a long time, Jake Murphy was truly speechless. He hadn't been expecting that.

16

SURVIVOR CAMP #3, EL PASO, TEXAS
OCTOBER 23RD

"Are you sure, sir? I know what Sidney says, but she's a civilian."

Jake nodded and gestured with his head back toward the camp. "It's worse than I thought, Sergeant."

He and Carmen stood on the gravel and dirt path that marked the perimeter of the camps, the line where residents were not allowed to pass. Jake had never agreed with allowing the refugees to keep their weapons for defense against the infected; now it was going to come back to bite them all in the ass.

He'd been stuck in the camp for almost two weeks, but not quite half of the time that Colonel Albrecht had sentenced him. In that time, he'd learned that the camp was one minor incident away from a full-on revolt. There were organized groups of armed men and women who'd been given missions to accomplish on the day the balloon went up. Everything from the overall plan to kill as many soldiers as possible, to very specific orders to infiltrate the division headquarters so they could kill the commanding general, and to eliminate the guards at the food warehouses. From what he could gather, Camp Three leaders were even in contact with resistance fighters in the other camps.

General Bhagat would get his wishes. There would be a massive reduction in the number of mouths to feed soon.

Staff Sergeant Wyatt exchanged a look with her companion, a tall, hulking soldier named Dickerson. A look passed between the two and Jake knew that they were more than just a squad leader and her soldier. "How bad, sir?" she asked.

"I'm not privy to the private meetings, just the camp scuttlebutt," he replied. "But it sounds like within a week, maybe less, they're gonna rise up."

"Maybe you should tell him," Dickerson rumbled. The sergeant shot him a withering glare that didn't deter him. "Sidney trusts him. Plus, he just gave us the best information out of anyone. It's time, Caitlyn."

Her eyes opened wide in shock. Jake groaned internally. As a soldier, he didn't approve of the relationship, but he didn't really care about it. She composed herself then turned her attention back to Carmen and Jake.

"What are you planning to do about the uprising, sir?"

"There's nothing I can do. Based on what I told Lieutenant Mirman a couple days ago, the security patrols have tripled in and around the camp—"

"Yeah, thanks for that," Sergeant Wyatt quipped.

"Sorry," he said. The twelve on, twelve off had changed to eighteen on, six off for the soldiers not on wall duty in order to make up for the additional workload. It wasn't sustainable, but for the short term, it was effective. "I don't have pull with anyone in the camp, I'm too new. Nobody trusts me yet, so if this thing goes off, I can't stop it."

The sergeant nodded. "Understood, sir. We— Goddamn it." She stopped and clenched her fists, a pained look on her face. "Fuck it. Sir, Me, Dickerson here, and Sidney are gonna leave Fort Bliss."

Her words were both alarming and a relief. On one hand, to hear her openly talk of desertion made him angry beyond belief. They were fighting for their lives every day against the infected, the loss of two combat soldiers wasn't significant, but it could have an impact in the long run. On the other hand, he'd had the same thoughts about leaving with Carmen and her children. The fact that others were thinking the same thing meant that he wasn't a horrible person.

"Sidney is eight or nine months pregnant," he stated.

Carmen shoved him. "Who's Sidney?"

"A friend," he stated, not wanting to go into the details of how Sidney was able to make it out of the camps. "She's pregnant."

"I'm a nurse," Carmen offered. "If she needs care, I did a six month rotation in Labor and Delivery. And I want to leave this camp too. The sooner the better."

Jake sighed. "I can't believe I'm going to say this to you, but..." *You're an officer dammit.* He warred with himself internally for a moment before finally admitting it aloud. "Carmen and I were planning to leave as well. I can't do anything while I'm stuck in here though."

"Well it sounds like you can't wait two more weeks," Sergeant Wyatt said.

"Yeah. I think this place is about to implode," he reconfirmed. "But what—"

"How serious are you about leaving the base, sir?"

He felt Carmen's fingers interlock with his, adding to his resolve. She'd committed herself to him, overcoming her original prejudices because of what happened at the warehouse. He was directly responsible for her and her two children, Patricia and Miguel, and needed to take whatever steps were necessary to ensure their survival.

"*Very*," he replied.

"Okay. The information you've given us about the situation in the camp has moved up our timeline by a couple of days," the sergeant stated. "But it's workable. The infected are the most active at night, so there's less scrutiny on the camps during the fighting. Can you meet us here at zero-four-hundred tonight?"

"You want to leave tonight?"

"We'll load everything we've set aside into our vehicle and pick you up, then stage until daylight.

I've got a good friend who's an RTO at the BDOC. He…owes me a favor. I'll make sure he's on shift tomorrow morning."

"What is a bee dock?" Carmen asked, repeating the word that Sergeant Wyatt used.

"The BDOC is the Base Defense Operations Center," Jake said. "And an RTO is the Radio Telephone Operator. The RTO takes the calls from the gate personnel. How can you be sure that he won't sell us out?"

"I have my ways," she purred.

Dickerson's lips thinned and Jake thought he understood what *her ways* were. "No way, Caitlyn."

"You knew how I was before we got together, Eric," Sergeant Wyatt said. "And this will help us get off the base. You got a better way?"

He stared off hard into the camp for a moment before saying, "No. This is the last time if we're going to make this work."

"We'll talk about that later," she answered.

"Yeah, we will," the private replied. He turned and stomped back toward the Stryker that he and Sergeant Wyatt had arrived in.

Jake didn't take his eyes off of Dickerson as he left. "Is he going to be a problem?" he asked. The private and the sergeant were fucking, that much was apparent. What was also apparent was that Dickerson took their relationship much more seriously than she did. As it stood, no one would stop them from leaving the base. That was every citizen's right, but they wouldn't have the truck or any of the military equipment that Sergeant Wyatt said she had stored up. They would leave on foot with the clothes on their backs.

"Dickerson?" Wyatt asked. "No, he'll get in line and do what I say."

"I don't know what your arrangement is—or isn't—with him, but our lives are literally depending on him keeping his cool for a few more hours," Jake stated.

"Don't worry, *sir*. He hates it inside these walls as much as we all do, and he's prepared to help us leave."

Jake glanced at Carmen, who nodded and said, "I know a thing or two about getting men to do what you want. That boy looks completely enamored with Caitlyn."

"Okay. What other choice do we have?" Jake grumbled. "I'm stuck in the camps for at least two more weeks anyways, even if I think this thing is going to explode before then."

The conversation died away after that, causing Sergeant Wyatt to shift uncomfortably from foot to foot. "Alright, I'm gonna head back to the barracks," she said. "I've got some work to do."

Jake reached out to shake her hand and then thought better of it in case anyone was watching from the camp. As it was, they could easily explain away the meeting with the soldiers as requesting supplies of some sort. People did that all the time, even if they rarely got anything from it. "Do you have—ah, do you have a couple of tampons?" Jake asked tentatively.

"What?"

"Tampons," he repeated. "That'd be a good excuse for why we're over here talking to you."

"Uh…sure. I always keep a few in my pouch, just in case." She reached behind her and pulled the buttpack around from where it rested below her vest. Inside, she dug two plastic-wrapped tubes out and handed them to Carmen.

"Thanks," the Latino replied.

"Yeah. I should probably grab a few boxes of those to take with us, huh?"

Carmen nodded. "Probably."

"Okay, I'll see you guys here at four a.m., right?"

"Absolutely," Jake said. "We'll have Carmen's two children with us. Will your truck be big enough to hold us all?"

She grinned back at him, then pointed at the Stryker behind her. "We're taking *that*, sir. We'll have room."

"You're stealing a Stryker?"

"Yup. And, now that you're coming along, I can be the gunner while you TC."

The mention of her being the gunner reminded him of Corporal Jones. He'd be a good guy to have along. "Do you think my gunner Corporal Jones would leave with us? He's enthusiastic about Sidney's proposal to remain silent and let the infected fade back into the desert, so he may be willing to take the next step."

"We don't have a lot of time to be making additions to the group, but I'll try to feel him out," Wyatt said.

"Thanks. Alright, see you tonight, Sergeant."

Carmen's fingers interlaced with his once more as he watched the soldier depart. "Come on, Jake. We need to get ready."

"*Shh, shh, Chiquita,*" Carmen shushed her daughter as she woke her. "Momma is going to take you to the bathroom.

"But I don't need to go potty," the girl protested.

Jake watched silently as he shifted the boy, Miguel, in his arms. Their noise discipline would be the key to making it out of the camp without raising an alarm. Most everyone was asleep, but with this many people, and the gunfire on the walls only a half mile or so from where they were, *someone* was guaranteed to be awake.

"I know, baby. But we gotta try so you don't pee pee in the bed again." That last part would hopefully deter anyone who'd heard their movements from noticing they both wore backpacks filled with all of their worldly belongings.

She picked up her daughter and the blanket she'd been wrapped in. With a nod from her, Jake turned and picked his way over the sleeping bodies on the tent floor.

They moved quickly toward the appointed meeting spot, a stretch of gravel roughly centered between two of the normal parking spots for military vehicles on the edge of camp. Behind them, on top of the wall, soldiers fired into the mobs of infected that were attracted to the base lights every night.

Occasionally, large gouts of yellow flame lit the sky, sending Jake and Carmen's shadows racing in front of them before fading away.

It wasn't easy to navigate the gutters, detritus, and sleeping forms without causing an alarm, but somehow, they made it to the link up point. Jake directed Carmen to stay in the shadows with the two kids while he walked forward to the edge of the gravel.

A searchlight illuminated immediately as the rocks crunched beneath his feet. A speaker mounted on the front of a Humvee fifty yards away crackled to life. *"Return to the camp."*

Jake stopped and raised his hands above his head, but did not turn back. He knew one of the soldiers would leave the vehicle and approach him if he just stayed put. That was the brigade's standard operating procedure as a way of de-escalating a potentially problematic situation.

"Return to camp or you will be fired upon."

Still he waited with his hands raised into the air unthreateningly, but strategically positioned to shade his eyes from the bright searchlight. After a moment, he heard the creak of the armored vehicle's door open and then the soft *thud* as it closed.

"Sir, you can't leave the camp. It's not safe here. You have to return."

"Not safe my ass," he muttered.

"What's that?"

He allowed his hand to drop slightly so the soldier could see his face. "Oh. Sorry, sir. I didn't know it was you," the man replied.

"It's alright, Specialist Mitchell" he said, dropping his hands completely so the medic could see him. "Staff Sergeant Wyatt is supposed to pick me and my informant up at zero four hundred. Have you seen her?"

"No, sir," Mitchell replied. "I, ah… I thought you had another two weeks or so, sir."

"I did, but that woman," he gestured to where Carmen stood in the shadows, "has information about the resistance that Colonel Albrecht needs to know about. I coordinated with Sergeant Wyatt today for the pick-up."

"We didn't hear anything about it."

"Of course you didn't, Specialist." Twin headlights in the distance brought his eyes up over the medic's shoulder. "Looks like that's her."

Mitchell turned and nodded. "Sure, that's a Stryker, sir. But I can't let you past me. You know that."

Jake ignored him and waved Carmen over. She walked awkwardly, carrying Patricia as Miguel stumbled along, holding her waist. When she was a few feet away, Jake walked casually to her and picked up the boy. "Just go with it," he whispered, catching the almost imperceptible dip of her chin.

"*She's* an informant?" Mitchell asked.

"Yeah," Jake replied, looking once again at the Stryker vehicle that was still about a quarter of a mile away.

"I don't know, sir. I think I may need to get Sergeant Turner. He's a few trucks over. Can you wait here?"

"No, goddammit!" Jake hissed. ""Everyone in that goddamned camp has seen me leading this woman to a group of soldiers. She'd be dead within a few hours."

"It's not that I don't believe you, sir. I just can't authorize her leaving—or you for that matter."

The Stryker stopped and he heard the locks on the vehicle's back ramp disengage. Then the ramp began to lower slowly. "I'm not going to risk this woman's life," the lieutenant barked. "She has information about the resistance and they are ready to strike against the military in a couple of hours."

"What?" Mitchell asked in shock. "Sir, I—"

"Damned right, you didn't know." Jake grunted, bulling his way past the medic to the back of the Stryker. Behind him, he heard the gravel crunching as Carmen hurried after him.

"Sir. Sir! What am I supposed to do here?" Specialist Mitchell asked.

Jake turned back to him. "Tell Sergeant Turner to rouse the CO and meet me at the company in twenty minutes. Then we'll all go see the brigade commander and let him know about the resistance."

He felt more than a little bit ashamed for lying to the young man and worse that he was going to abandon his brothers in arms. He'd tried to rationalize it in his mind that their position was unsustainable, and therefore it should be abandoned before the entire human race was destroyed. Besides, it wasn't like he was going to a magical safe haven. He'd likely be killing hundreds of infected outside of the camp over the course of the next few days trying to make it out of the city.

"Hey, Mitchell."

"Yes, sir?" Mitchell replied.

"Do me a favor and keep clear of the camps, okay? This is gonna go bad really quickly. They're armed to the teeth and pissed off. They won't care if you're trying to save someone's life. Understood?"

"I have to go with my platoon, sir. *Our* platoon."

"I know, but keep your head down. Can you promise me that?"

"Yes, sir," the medic replied, smiling hesitantly.

Jake bit back a tear, both for the lives that would probably be lost to this insanity and for his own cowardice at leaving his men before things went to shit. Regardless of how much he told himself he wasn't, that was exactly how he felt.

He was a coward.

17

NEAR TYRONE, OKLAHOMA
OCTOBER 24TH

"Damn. That was good while it lasted," Tim groaned, shutting the bedroom door on the remains of their pet.

"What's wrong?" Russ asked, concern lacing his words. He was in the farmhouse's kitchen cooking a slab of bacon and a few eggs for their morning meal.

"Luwanda."

A fork clattered to the counter and Tim appeared a few seconds later. He glanced back and forth between the closed door and the look that must have been evident on Tim's face. "Is she…"

"Yeah. I guess she starved to death or something. Who the fuck knows with those things?"

A small sob escaped his lips. Tim knew that his brother had cared for the looney, way more than was healthy. "Come here, big fella. It'll be alright."

Russ fell into his arms as Tim hugged him. "We'll get us another one."

"Luwanda was special though. I think she liked me. I mean, in her own way."

Tim patted the other man's back dutifully, even if he *did* think that he was being a melodramatic loser. Maybe he was having such a hard time with this one because she lasted so long. They'd had her, *what*, a month, month-and-a-half? During that time, Russ had developed an odd bond with the infected female. He'd caught the other man in the bedroom talking to her as if she could respond on several occasions. It wasn't healthy. The infected they captured, prepared, and cleaned up were supposed to simply be a living, breathing sex toy whose bodies still responded in natural ways to stimulation. That's it. They weren't supposed to be anything else, especially not a goddamned girlfriend or whatever Russ thought it was.

"Okay, Russ. She's dead," he said, pushing the other man away. He was done comforting him. "It happens every time. They just don't live long without eating…well, whatever the fuck they're all eating out there in the wild."

The bigger man wiped at his eyes as he sat on a bench in the foyer. "I think I need a few days before we get another one."

Tim nodded. "That's okay, brother. We can give it a rest. We probably need to go raid the pharmacy in town for more condoms and penicillin anyways."

"So what are we gonna do with her body?"

"We can do whatever you need, buddy. The easiest thing would be to throw her in the kill pit and burn her like we've done with all the others." He sighed. "But I know she was special to you."

Russ considered it for a while until the smell of smoke from the kitchen made him jump up from the seat. He ran across the small space to the kitchen and soon began cursing.

Tim walked into the kitchen idly, preferring the other man deal with the smoke and the mess. "Bacon's burnt," he said, pointing to the frying pan on the stove.

"I know," Russ grumbled. "It's not *really* burnt though, so it should be okay."

"Alright then," he replied, picking up a plate from the counter and wiping away the crumbs from last night's meal. "So, what do you want me to do with Luwanda's body?"

Russ looked up at him, chewing on a crunchy piece of bacon. "Burn it. She wasn't nothing but a looney that we used to get our rocks off."

Tim raised an eyebrow. "You sure? 'Cause five minutes ago, you was saying how much she meant to you and all."

"We'll get a new one," the big man said. "Maybe we can figure out how to keep the next one alive."

"I've been thinking about that."

"What'd you come up with?"

"What if we don't get another one?"

"Goddammit, Tim. You know I need a release that jerking off just don't satisfy. I need—"

"Shut up and let me finish. Damn, you're impatient sometimes. It ain't like we've got anywhere to be. You don't gotta be at the shop to earn money or nothing."

"You're right," Russ said, properly rebuked. "I just don't know what you mean. I thought we agreed that keeping a woman around was best for both of us."

"It is. But I'm done with having to keep gloves on a looney's hands and making sure her mouth is taped up properly. Worrying about getting blood on me from all those wounds that won't heal up. Hell, I'm *done* with wearing a whole bunch of condoms. I barely feel any of it."

"What do you want to do, then?"

"Let's get us a live one." Russ stared at him in confusion so he clarified. "I mean, a woman who's not infected. There's that other camp on the west side of Liberty. They've got women. We should take one of them."

"We can't just take one of their women, Tim. Old Man Campbell will come looking for her."

Tim shrugged. After the hell that they'd lived through, he wasn't concerned with old Vern Campbell. The infected were slowly thinning out in the area, so maybe it was time they started preparing for the future.

The old farmhouse they lived in had been well provisioned and the solar panels generated more than enough electricity for just the two of them, but after seven months, the freezers were slowly starting to empty. It was time the brothers began to seriously contemplate rationing or supplementing their mostly meat diet with shelf-stable products from the grocery store. Those damn Campbells had made it their mission to clean out the stores and take everything to their farm. They'd run into one another on various supply runs, each group warily watching the other.

"Maybe there will be an "accident" the next time we run into them," Tim stated. "Maybe they get rolled up by a group of infected and we get their women."

"Go on," Russ prompted, obviously warming to the idea.

"Maybe we just take what we want, kill the men and burn the bodies. Old Vern will be none the wiser and just think that his people got infected and runned off chasing noises like the rest of them."

"I been eying that Sally Campbell for years," Russ replied. "You think we could grab her?"

"If she's one of the ones who shows up, yeah. If not, even that other granddaughter, the brunette—"

"Katie."

"Yeah. She's a looker." Tim slapped the table. "Think about *that*. I imagine they'd appreciate a little action."

"I could give Sally *a lot* of action," Russ said, his eyes glazing over as he was already thinking about what he'd do to her.

"It's settled then. We gotta do some housekeeping here, clean out that bedroom and all. We also need to finish mending that fence where those four infected got tangled up yesterday. Plus, it's maintenance day for the solar panels and the battery bank. After that, we can plan our next move."

Russ nodded enthusiastically. "I'll go get the wheelbarrow so we can take out the *trash*."

"Good man," Tim said, leaning back to pat his stomach. "Maybe that Miss Sally will even do some of the cookin' and cleanin' around this place. Lord knows it ain't had a good scrubbing since Momma died."

The mention of their mother sobered up his younger brother, as Tim knew it would. There was a lot of work to do today before they got lost planning their ambush.

18

OUTSIDE OF TUCUMCARI, NEW MEXICO
OCTOBER 28TH

"What do you think, Sergeant?" Jake asked. He'd considered moving past the military rank structure since they'd gone AWOL, but so far, it had stuck.

She handed the binoculars back to him. "I don't know. Looks empty, like they all left, but that's probably not the case."

"Yeah, I doubt it too. It's a really warm day today, maybe the infected are staying in the shadows."

"Maybe. We could just drive up through town and see what we scare up."

"I don't know what you two are discussing," Carmen called from down inside the troop compartment. "But Sidney and I could both use a bath and that lake on the other side of town is just what we need."

Jake glanced at his gunner, Sergeant Wyatt, and grinned. He'd known what the women down below wanted to do from the moment they'd seen the large body of water on the map. The general lack of hygiene is all the two non-military women had talked about after only a few hours inside the Stryker's belly when they left El Paso five days ago.

They'd followed Highway 54 the entire way so far. Partly because it was an even, paved road headed away from the Safe Zone, but primarily because it went through a bunch small towns, avoiding cities that would have had a large pre-outbreak population. Even with that strategy, they'd had a couple of close calls in several of those small towns. The infected were a constant threat that always seemed to appear at the most inconvenient times—like when Miguel had gotten diarrhea and was shitting into an MRE box behind the truck. Two hundred infected pressed around a buttoned-up vehicle was a pain in the ass to move through, even with a .50 caliber machine gun taking out the edges of the crowd. Everything else was below the gun's angle and had to be dealt with by rocking the vehicle back and forth, crushing bodies each time and wasting a lot of fuel.

"Ahh, the simpler times," he muttered.

"What's that, sir?" Wyatt asked.

"Oh, nothing. I was just thinking about better days."

"Okay. Great," she replied in frustration. "What do you want to do about the town? Do we stay on 54 and go right through the center of town, or do we try to bypass it?"

Jake considered the options. Bypassing it meant going on Interstate 40 to the south and then they could decide to stay on it and go back into Texas around Amarillo, which meant *not* going to the lake. The women would strangle him for doing that; Carmen might *actually* physically lay hands on him. There wasn't a necessary advantage over bypassing the town, other than it had a population of about 5,500 people before the virus according to the little town data section. Certainly not all of those people would have wandered off.

"Any hits on thermal?" he asked, trying to arm himself with more information.

The sergeant dropped down and the .50 caliber began to rotate slowly beside him on the right. After a moment, Wyatt popped back up. "Nothing, sir."

"Hey, Dickerson," Jake said into his mic. "Honk the horn a few times."

Dickerson responded immediately, pressing the horn rapidly for several weak blasts, then holding it down. Jake also grabbed the microphone for the loudspeaker mounted on the vehicle and whistled long and loud. "That'll get something moving," he remarked.

"Contact!" Sergeant Wyatt shouted.

Jake saw them. There were about ten infected that emerged slowly from various buildings at the edge of town, the closest was about two hundred meters away. All of them were a pathetic excuse for human beings. He'd seen their kind sprinkled amongst the average attackers back at Bliss: emaciated, diseased, barely upright due to lack of calories. They shuffled forward quickly rather than running at a full sprint like most of the infected he'd dealt with.

If he was being generous, he'd say it was a jog.

"I'm gonna try to take them out with the M-2010," Jake said calmly as he pulled the suppressed sniper rifle up through the hatch.

"Got it, sir. I'll continue to scan. Engagement orders?"

"I want to keep it quiet, so give me an opportunity to get rid of these guys first."

"Understood."

Jake settled the rifle into the pocket of his shoulder and leaned forward across the top of the Stryker, using the roof as a base for his elbow. Peering through the scope, he sighted in on the closest of the infected, surprised to see that what had been two hundred meters was less than a hundred now. These things' slow, but unyielding pace was deceiving.

He fired, hitting the infected square in the chest. It faltered, then fell, tumbling forward several feet. He knew that .300 WinMag round might not kill the thing, but the massive exit it would likely cause would take it out of the fight until it did die.

He opened his non-firing eye and scanned the area in front of him as he racked the bolt, cycling a new round. When he decided which of the fast walkers was the next threat, he focused in on a woman. She shambled quickly, practically windmilling her arms to give her more momentum to increase her speed. He took steady aim and hit her high in the chest, near her throat. The impact of the bullet knocked her upper body backward as her lower half continued to move toward him, her feet lifting off the ground. He watched until she fell onto her back and then began to seek a new target.

Jake quickly went through the five rounds in the magazine, plus the one in the chamber when he started, and switched to a new one. He burned through those just as quickly and accepted his first magazine back from Sergeant Wyatt, who'd reloaded it for him.

Two more shots and the threat at the edge of town was eliminated. "Nice shooting, sir."

He smiled and glanced at the NCO. Her eyes sparkled with a little bit more than appreciation. "Thank you, Sergeant. I was on the rifle team in college." Jake coughed uncomfortably, then said, "Let's reload the M-2010 magazines and try to draw some more of them out."

After a second series of horn blasts and whistles, they got three more of the infected to emerge from buildings or alleyways farther away, which Jake was able to dispatch quickly. They repeated the process again and Jake shouted into the microphone, but no other infected appeared.

"Okay, I think we're clear up here," Jake declared after a full ten minutes of fruitless observation. "Dickerson, how's your fuel?"

"One-quarter of a tank, sir."

"Alright, that's good enough. Let's move forward—slowly."

Dickerson shifted the Stryker into gear and began to creep forward. He swerved left and right a few times to crush the bodies of any infected still moving, despite their critical injuries. When they were about a hundred meters from the town, Jake sank down inside the vehicle, closing the hatch above him.

He watched through the viewports for movement while Sergeant Wyatt scanned with the TWS. The dusty town, nothing more than a collection of single-story buildings and homes, passed by quickly without any further incident.

"Stop!" the gunner announced when they'd passed what Jake estimated to be the halfway point of town.

"What is it?"

"You have got to take a look at this, sir."

He maneuvered inside the vehicle until he was looking over her shoulder at the monitor. "Are those? Zoom in."

She complied, zooming the camera until the indistinct mounds became clearer. "Looks like bones to me, sir."

"Yeah… Do a quick thermal scan. See if we can see anything."

She rotated the thermal camera and weapon's platform slowly in a 360-degree circle. "Everything looks clear as far as I can tell, Lieutenant."

"Fuck," Jake muttered, dreading what he was about to say. "Give the horn a few blasts, Dickerson. Let's draw 'em out."

The private did as ordered and Sergeant Wyatt continued to scan for heat signatures. Nothing happened, so Jake shouted a bunch of jumbled nonsense into the loudspeaker. Still nothing.

"I'm gonna go check it out."

"What the fuck did you just say, sir?"

"I'm… I'm gonna go check out those bones. That's not normal and we need to know what the hell we're dealing with."

"Normal?" she scoffed. "None of this is normal. I don't like you leaving the vehicle."

"I'm sorry you don't like it, Sergeant. But if we're going to survive on our own out here, we need to understand these things better than just reacting to them every time they show up."

"This is my vehicle, *sir*." That last word was practically a hiss. "Who's to say I won't leave you if you get out?"

He turned to her. "Is that how this is gonna be? Are we done pretending the rank structure still exists?"

"*Hey!*" Carmen shouted from below, slapping his leg. "You two quit measuring your dicks. We need both of you."

"I'm fine with you being the lieutenant," Wyatt said, ignoring Carmen's statement. "You asked to join me. You would have been stuck on that base if it wasn't for me and what I had to do to get the RTO to lie about our authorization to leave."

"Don't bring that into it. You enjoyed it."

"Maybe so," she responded, her eyes blazing. "But we have this vehicle because of me. This is my vehicle and I don't want *you* to leave it. It's not safe. We're in the middle of a goddamned town."

Jake could tell that she wasn't going to budge without him explaining what he was thinking. "Look, Wyatt—Caitlyn," he added for a more personal feel. "I understand what you're saying, and if you want to be in charge, fine. I really don't care. But I have a responsibility to Carmen and those two kids to keep them safe, for the long term, not just today, or the next few days. Those piles of bones represent a potential glimpse into how these things function, what they do when they're not hunting humans. The more we understand their behavior, the better off we'll be when we get to wherever we're going for the long term."

Her expression had softened somewhat as he talked. He'd surprised himself when he told her that she could be in charge. It wasn't something that he'd thought about, but in reality, he really didn't care. He just wanted to keep everyone safe.

"Sir, I—"

"It's Jake. I think we've moved past the rank thing."

"Okay. Jake. I don't disagree with you. Understanding your enemy is always a good thing, but this is dangerous. We're in the middle of nowhere, with no back up, and no chance of medical aid if something happens. It's not safe."

"We were on our own the moment we left those gates," he replied. "We won't be safe for a long time. As long as we're out here on the road, not inside some type of safe house or compound, then we're in danger. And if one of us needs medical attention from a wound sustained from the infected, then the only remedy is a bullet in the brain."

"Dammit, you're putting me in a shitty position," Caitlyn stated. "If you get yourself killed, then I'm responsible for the safety of everyone in this truck."

"You already are, Caitlyn. I'm not planning on getting myself killed. That's why I've been making sure we're alone before I step foot off the Stryker." He paused for a breath, then said, "We need to understand them if we're going to survive. This is a perfect opportunity. All of them are dead or gone. We might not ever get this chance again."

The emotions warred across her face. Finally, she nodded. "Hold on. I want to scan the area a few more times." Without waiting for an answer, she dropped down and began to turn the weapons platform. It made three slow rotations before she reappeared.

"I don't see anything. If you're going, you'd better do it now."

"You promise you're not going to drive off and leave me?" he asked, grinning.

"No. I might leave you just out of spite."

Jake pressed his hands against the roof of the Stryker and jumped up, setting his butt on the edge of the TC hatch. Then he swung his legs up and out of the vehicle. Finally, he lay on his stomach and reached inside, retrieving the M-4 that Wyatt had gotten for him from somewhere.

"I'll be back in a few minutes." He scooted down past the driver's hatch, which Dickerson had open now.

"Good luck, sir."

"Thanks, Eric," he said, letting the private know that he was on a first name basis now too. With only the three of them, who were no longer technically in the Army, it didn't make any sense to keep it up.

What the hell? Jake asked himself as he tried to make sense of what he saw.

It was only in the high 60s, but his adrenaline was kicked up and making him sweat. He wiped the perspiration away from his forehead quickly and then returned his hand to the barrel guard of his M-4. Scanning the four massive mounds of bones, he decided there wasn't any threat, but there were two darkened doorways leading into the building on the left.

He moved as far across the alleyway as possible and glanced back at the Stryker. Eric Dickerson was raised out of the driver's hatch, his own rifle trained on the alley where Jake stood. The .50 cal on top was currently facing away from him as Wyatt rotated it slowly in a circle looking for targets.

With his back-up as firm as it could be, given the circumstances, he slipped the night vision monocular down over his eye. He'd chosen the monocular from Wyatt's pilfered inventory because it gave him the option to use the night vision or his naked eye, switching back and forth as needed without a lot of extra movements. Walking quickly to the first opening, he began using a single person room clearing technique known as slicing the pie.

He put his back against the wall and then turned to face the doorway. He used the barrel of his rifle as a guide, keeping it pointed into to darkness as he took one step away from the building. When he switched on the monocular, he closed his opposite eye and searched the green-lit room for any more of the infected. When he was satisfied that there wasn't anything immediately threatening in the corner that he could see, he began to advance, his feet tracing the line of a shallow arc from one side of the doorway to the other while his rifle remained trained on the area inside. As he advanced, he rotated his body so that by the time he was on the far side of the door, he was basically facing back the way he'd just come from.

There were more bodies inside the room. They were unmoving and appeared to be missing pieces and parts. These were more than just bones—although, he'd glimpsed many of those in his quick clearing. He wanted to investigate, but there was another threat less than twenty feet away that needed to be cleared before he could examine the contents of the room.

He cleared the next room in the same manner, by slicing the pie. The odor emanating from it made him wonder if he'd stumbled upon a sewage treatment plant. When he was satisfied that nothing was an immediate threat, he flipped the monocular up and turned on the flashlight mounted to the side of his M-4. Besides his pistol and the knife on his vest, it was the only piece kit that he wore that had originally belonged to him. He'd taken the flashlight with him into the refugee camp for emergency illumination. It was bright enough to illuminate the front porch of a neighbor's house at 150 feet—he'd tried it often.

The inside of the room was covered with filth. Excrement seemed to be everywhere, the floors, the walls, even the ceiling had a healthy amount of it up there. That was the only feature of the room besides piles of rags in each of the corners. Jake wondered if the rags were where the infected slept, like a nest. Every animal in nature made sleeping areas of some type, were the infected simply more like animals than humans now?

He walked back to the alley and switched off his light until the next room, where he turned it back on to get a better view of the inside. He was shocked to see the condition of the bodies that he'd glimpsed when he cleared the room quickly before. There were the bones that he'd noticed, strewn haphazardly around the space, but there were also full bodies, at least ten or more. From the alleyway, it looked as if the bodies were being eaten. Consumed for their meat.

The corpses all appeared to be emaciated, like the ones they'd killed on the outskirts of town. "Holy shit. That's how they're staying alive," he mumbled, startling himself at how loud his whisper sounded in the total silence of the alley. The infected were eating their dead.

The stench emanating from the room was horrendous. It was a mixture of rotten meat, feces, stale urine, blood, and twenty other odors that he couldn't identify. Jake took a deep breath and adjusted his t-shirt up over his nose before stepping inside, careful to avoid touching the bodies or accidentally stepping in a pile of excrement.

He didn't need to see much, but he did want to verify that all of the bodies were from the infected. It only took a few glances to confirm his suspicion, and then he was back in the alley. The dead all appeared to be the infected. They were mostly nude with cracked and bloody fingernails, had sunken eyes, scabs everywhere, and patches of missing hair where it fell out from poor nutrition and likely from their own yanking of it in their insanity.

The town was fairly isolated, with the nearest small town about seven miles away across an unforgiving desert in the summertime. The infected that stayed in the town probably ate through everything edible they could find and then began to turn on each other. The weaker ones were probably the first to go and the ten or fifteen he'd killed were the last remaining residents of Tucumcari, New Mexico.

Jake scanned the area again to make sure there weren't any threats and then returned to the Stryker. After giving a quick back brief to everyone inside, they continued down Highway 54 to the lake, where they repeated the horn and loudspeaker method to draw out any infected that might be lingering there.

With no threats in the area, Jake and Caitlyn authorized the civilians to bathe in the water while one of the soldiers maintained security at all times. The women were directed to stay nearby, in eye contact of each other and the Stryker so they could respond to any threats.

As the women splashed in the lake, Jake couldn't help but notice how thin Sidney was compared to Carmen's shapely body. She had tattoos covering her arms and a few on her upper back. She was an attractive woman with a razor's wit that kept him thinking every time he spoke with her.

Even with her protruding belly, he felt himself becoming attracted to the pregnant woman. She laughed and splashed some water at Miguel in response to something he said. She glanced sideways at Jake sitting atop the vehicle and smiled, her lips revealing straight, white teeth. Then she turned away to begin washing away the dust and grime of the road.

19

NEAR LIBERAL, KANSAS
OCTOBER 29TH

Sally yawned, stretching her hands above her head until they reached the headboard. It felt good to work out the soreness in her shoulders. Over the past month, they'd harvested the crops and preserved everything that they could in various manners from canning to dehydrating and freezing. This week was all about cutting down the plants and corn stalks for use as feed for their small herd.

Grandpa refused to let them use the tractor for fear of attracting the infected. It was hard work with the primitive tools they used and her hands were covered in burst blisters where callouses hadn't formed yet. She wondered if they'd had the right tools for the job, then would the work have been as difficult. If they'd owned some type of pioneer-style farming tools, then they wouldn't have had to use hoes and shovels to cut the corn stalks. Her grandfather assured her that they'd use the tractor to till the ground in the spring, five months from now, but it didn't help ease the soreness she felt.

It made sense. In another five months, the infected should be pretty well cleared out of the area. They'd only had three show up during the entire harvest, so the harsh plains winter would probably kill most of them that were out wandering around without any clothing.

She glanced at her cell phone. It was plugged into the wall, charging off the home's solar power. There had been some attempts by the federal government to get the Internet back up and running, but it was mostly just broadcasts about what to do against the infected and safety procedures—as if anyone reading those announcements today wouldn't have already figured it out months ago. She hadn't been as ditsy as her sister, but Sally still missed her daily dose of pop culture via the web.

A soft tapping on her door brought her back to reality. It was probably Katie or Grandpa telling her it was time to wake up and get ready for the day. "Yeah?" she asked, her voice scratchy from sleep.

"I'm sorry to bother you, Miss Sally," Jesse said. "But there's a whole mess of infected coming down the road and we need all the help we can get."

She sat up, her sheets falling away to reveal that she only wore a t-shirt under the covers. She snatched the blankets up quickly, then chuckled at her embarrassment since the door was clearly closed. "What's a whole mess mean, Jesse?" she asked, putting her feet over the side of the bed onto the old wooden floors.

"They're still about a mile out, but best we can tell, there's about fifty of 'em. They's still too far to shoot with that suppressed rifle of John's so Mr. Campbell wants us to go out and take care of 'em."

"*Fifty!* Wow. That's crazy. What are so many of them doing out there?" She was already pulling on her jeans.

"I don't rightly know, ma'am. They all just appeared over the hill, travelin' south down Zielne Road."

"South?" she asked, pausing as she pulled her nightshirt over her head. "Why are they coming from up north?" For months, the infected had only come *from* the south, along Highway 54, and from the east, where Liberal was. They hadn't seen anything coming southward in forever.

"Not sure, ma'am. There's no tellin' where this group come from. They coulda wandered west out of Liberal and then turned down Zielne at the sound of the cattle this mornin'."

Sally opened the door, startling poor Jesse. "Oh, sorry."

He grinned. "S'okay, ma'am. I'm used to gettin' a fright these days."

"Well, I didn't mean to, okay? Where's Grandpa?"

"He's down in the kitchen, eatin' a biscuit from last night's supper."

"Alright. Thank you, Jesse. I assume you're supposed to get Katie up as well?"

"Yes'm," he replied, ducking his head. The farmhand was as sweet as could be, but there wasn't a lot going on between his ears.

"You go wake her up and I'll go talk to Grandpa."

She didn't wait for him to reply, choosing to bound down the stairs in excitement. *Fifty infected!* It would be like a battle royale in one of those video games her old boyfriend used to play. Only this was real life, not some silly game.

The thought of people from her old life sobered her up as she hit the first floor landing. The old floorboards creaked in protest to the sudden addition of weight.

"Now, don't go tearing my house up, child!" Grandpa chided her from the next room.

"Jesse told me about the horde," she exclaimed breathlessly. "What are we gonna do?"

"Well, we have a contingency plan for things like this," he replied. "You already know that we have that barbed wire beside the road, ready to stretch into place. We just leave it down in case cars or something come by."

"That hasn't happened in *months*, maybe not even in a half a year," she reminded him.

"Well, we can always be hopeful that the government is actually doing something like they say they are in that broadcast. Anyways, I had Jesse and Scott stretch that wire across the road, to stop them. Once they get themselves all tangled up, then we go up and knock them upside the head, just like we do at the back forty fence. Easy as pie."

Sally nodded her head and pulled a biscuit from the pan that someone had reheated on the stove. As she chewed, a thought occurred to her. "Grandpa?"

"Yes, dear?"

"The fences in the fields that we rely on are secured to metal poles every eight or ten feet."

"Depending on the field, sure," he replied.

"So that keeps the wire in place. There's nothing like that on the wire across the road. What's gonna keep them from just piling up on top of the wire to collapse it and then the other infected will just walk across the ones that are tangled up?"

"Hmmm... Like the gooks used to do in 'Nam," he grunted, still clinging to old racial slurs, regardless of how much the girls told him that he shouldn't say them anymore. "They would have two or three privates throw themselves on the concertina wire and then the rest of 'em would run across their backs. That's some damn fine thinking, girl."

"So what do we do about it?"

"Well, we gotta get to them before they get to us now, don't we?"

"I, uh... I guess so."

"You eat some breakfast, get your energy up. We're gonna be doing a lot of close-in work this morning that will use up your reserves pretty damn quick."

Sally smirked. "Remember when we were kids and you used to say "PDQ" instead of actually saying the words? What happened?"

Grandpa pushed himself up from the table. "The Good Lord told me that a few little words won't mean much during the Trials of the Tribulation. And this, missy, is a very big trial." He pulled his old Carhart jacket on. "Did Jesse wake up Katie like I asked him to?"

"I think so. He was headed to her room when I came downstairs."

"Good. I want her up in the lookout stand so John can help us down on the ground."

"What about mom?"

He shrugged. "She's as useless during all this as she always is. Maybe she can make us some lunch so we can go right from killin' and haulin' bodies to haulin' corn stalks for the cattle."

"When do you *ever* get to take a rest on this old farm, Grandpa?"

Sally and her grandfather both turned to regard Katie, who'd just asked the question from the doorway. "Well, now, look who decided to finally get out of bed."

"Ha ha," Katie groaned. "Seriously, I need a day off."

"You'll get a day off when you're dead—Uh, sorry, girls. I didn't mean it like that."

"We know, Grandpa," Sally assured him. "We appreciate everything you're teaching us. It's a lot of work, but when we're all bundled up this winter with a nice, hot stew to eat, it'll be worth it."

Grandpa leaned over and kissed Sally's forehead. "That's my girl. I'm gonna go check on the boys' hasty fence work before that mob gets here. Katie, I need you to go up and tell John that I need him down on the ground. You're gonna go up there and keep an eye on things from up high. It's important that you watch in all directions, not just what's going on down at the road. We don't need a bunch more infected to show up behind us while we're dealing with the first group. Got it?"

"Yeah. I got it," Sally's younger sister replied.

Grandpa kissed her on the forehead as well. "Good girl. Now grab some breakfast so you can eat while you're up there on the lookout stand."

He walked over to the door and picked up the battered ballpeen hammer, his weapon of choice. "See you in a few minutes, Sally. Send Jesse out when you see him."

"These things are pathetic," Scott said, not meaning it as an insult. The mass of infected stretched across the road near the Campbell farm were in a truly sorry state. They all appeared to have suffered severe trauma, from broken hands and fingers to missing teeth.

"What *is* that?" Sally asked, thwacking what used to be a man against the side of his head with her bat. "I mean, why are all of their teeth missing?"

"Maybe they fell out because of poor nutrition," Grandpa offered as he sunk his hammer three inches into the top of a head, causing it to collapse when the shards of skull pierced its brain. "Or maybe they were holed up in a chemical factory that caused their teeth to fall out."

"It's just weird," Sally huffed, pushing her victim back with the end of the bat.

The infected were spread out along the thirty feet of fence. Parts of it were already beginning to collapse. It wouldn't take much more for the fence to fall down completely, and then they were done for.

They fought valiantly, dispatching probably half of the infected when the first disaster struck. Jesse cried out, then pitched forward into the fence. Less than a second later the report of a gun echoed across the plains. Sally turned, staring up at the lookout nest where Katie was supposed to be. She wasn't there.

"What the—"

Another gunshot sounded, impossibly loud after all the months of remaining silent. Scott was down, the infected in front of him tried unsuccessfully to grasp him with broken fingers.

"Run!" Grandpa shouted. "Get back to the house!"

Sally hesitated, looking at Jesse and Scott. "We can't—"

"They're gone," he yelled, grabbing her jacket and pulling her off balance. His strength surprised her, giving her no option but to follow or fall.

She ran back toward the house. "What's happening?"

"It was a trap. Somebody—"

Grandpa stumbled and fell. Sally stopped and tried to pull him back up. A large red stain was already beginning to spread across his tan jacket near his stomach. "Leave me, girl," he hissed through clenched teeth. "Get to the safety of the house. Figure out where they're attacking from… Kill them."

"I can't leave you."

"Yes, you can. Now go!"

She leaned down to kiss him, tears blurring her vision. "I love you, Grandpa." She pushed herself up and turned back to the house, then stopped.

John stood less than twenty feet away with his hands raised in the air. Sally wiped her eyes. The blurry shape of two men swam into her view. Both had rifles raised, aiming at John. Sally jumped when one of them shot the farmhand without warning. His body fell limp immediately, meaning they'd shot him in the head.

She considered running back toward the line of infected or even into the fields beside the road, but she didn't stand a chance. She was ten feet from the nearest fence, and then it was a wide open space after the harvest. There was nowhere to hide.

If she didn't do something fast, they would kill her just like they did John. "Shit," she mumbled and turned to sprint toward the fields. She'd taken two, maybe three steps when she felt a sting in the back of her thigh. Her leg went numb, causing her to fall.

The pavement rushed up, and her face smacked against it, making her eyes water more than they already were. The numbing sensation spread up her leg into her stomach as she tried to crawl to the field. *Where is Katie?* she wondered. The girl should have been shooting at the men from the lookout.

"Here, dose her up with the chloroform while I go round up the livestock," one of the men ordered. She reached back, feeling a feather or something similar sticking from her leg.

"Aww, come on! We got what we came for, Tim. Can't we just leave those stupid things behind?"

The heel of a boot stomped down beside her face and she felt herself lifted upward as one of the attackers grabbed her by the collar. A dirty handkerchief appeared and the hand holding it clamped down tight across her nose and mouth. The awful smell of something sweet mixed with chemicals invaded her senses and she tried not to breathe.

"No, I ain't leavin' them, asshole. It took me forever to pull all their teeth. These things are perfect for defense."

"I'm gettin' real tired of you talkin' to me like that, Tim. One of these days—"

Sally thrashed her head violently, trying to break the hold that the man had on her, but it was no use. Her body forced her to take a deep breath, and then another.

"One of these days what, fucker? You wanna throw down with me?"

Slowly, her world faded to black.

20

HOOKER, OKLAHOMA
OCTOBER 29TH

"Alright, time to wake up," Jake called across the gas station where they'd taken shelter the night before.

With over five hundred miles under their belt, the Stryker needed fuel and the jerry cans they'd strapped to the hull were empty as well. The big truck took diesel, which there was plenty of at the Love's Travel Center near the little Oklahoma town of Hooker, so they decided that it was worth the risk to stop at the potentially crowded station.

It took a while for the soldiers to clear the parking lot, then the building itself, but it was worth it. They'd found very few of the infected, and only two of them inside, so the place was relatively untouched—by current standards. The fuel pumps were worthless without power, so Dickerson and Jake spent a good hour siphoning fuel from the tanks of the long-abandoned semi-trucks. The gas was old, but usable once they added fuel stabilizer that they found inside the station.

When Sidney had gone inside the building, she'd considered just going back to the Stryker to sleep. The food aisles of Love's were a mess. Anything that could be smelled through the packaging had been torn into by the infected trapped inside. Of course, that was *after* what they'd done to the Subway sandwich shop. Sidney had made the mistake of walking over there to look for supplies, but the smell drove her away. It looked like the infected had lived in Subway for several months before moving into the main travel center.

Sidney turned over, crinkling the air mattress underneath her as she did. It was a new addition to her belongings, something she'd picked from the shelf only ten feet away. She pushed herself up awkwardly and went to the glass doors where the sodas and bottled waters were. The urge to pee was not quite as strong as her need for some type of sugar at the moment. Inside, she pulled out a room temperature iced frappuccino drink and checked the expiration date. It was two months past the use by date. On any other product she wouldn't have cared, but the ingredients list said it contained reduced fat milk, which would be very bad for her and the baby if it was spoiled. She sighed and put it back, opting for a warm Dr. Pepper instead.

She sidestepped a couple of piles of feces in the aisle and pulled a sticky bun from the shelf. "Those things will go straight to your hips," Jake chuckled, startling her as he came up beside her.

"Have you seen my hips?" she asked. "I could probably eat a bunch of these things and still be okay."

"I think you look great."

"Mmm hmm," she mumbled. "How's Carmen, lover boy?"

"She's, ahh... She's good."

"What? I thought you two were a thing. Certainly seemed like it last night when you went to the showers."

He coughed. "We were checking to see if there was any water pressure."

"Was there?" she asked, already knowing the answer.

"No. The pipes must be burst somewhere."

"Then what took you guys so long?" she laughed.

"There was... Okay, we were making out. There, is that what you wanted to hear?"

Sidney patted her stomach. "I get it. Stress relief and boredom. Hell, Caitlyn and Eric are humping every time we stop." She leaned in close to him and whispered, "Be careful. She'll be after you before too long."

"Yeah, I kind of got that vibe."

She opened the sticky bun and bit into it. Pre-outbreak, she would have ripped off a piece at a time, but it was just easier this way so she didn't have to touch it. "So, what's on the agenda, boss man?"

"I really wish you'd stop calling me that," he groaned. She'd taken to referring to him as the boss man a few days ago. It got under his skin, so she kept at it.

"But you're our fearless leader," she mocked. "What would we do without your leadership, Jake?"

"Be stuck on Fort Bliss with the rest of them, waiting to die."

She'd struck a nerve and decided to rein it in. Sometimes she forgot that he was only twenty-three. "Hey, I'm sorry, Jake," she said, placing a hand on his forearm, which he'd crossed over his chest. "I'm just playing around. You're doing an amazing job keeping us safe."

"Thanks."

"Uh oh. One word answers." *Damn, he must be really pissed.* "Alright, I'll stop calling you boss man. There, does that make things better?"

He nodded, frowning. "I think we keep heading north. Winter should be particularly hard on the infected since they wander around outside. The further north we can go, the better."

"And you think staying on the highway is still the best bet?"

"Yeah. I think it's a good route because we haven't seen any survivors and hardly any infected along this road so far. They must have all gone toward the bigger population centers."

"Or they starved to death," she offered, remembering the images from the little lake town back in New Mexico.

"Yeah, maybe. We're getting into cattle country and farmland, so they can eat the animals and grasses to survive. It's not a pleasant way to live, but—"

"I stopped giving a shit about those things the moment Lincoln died," Sidney interrupted him, adding a little bit of steel to her voice.

"Sorry," he replied.

"Don't be. You didn't know him."

He shrugged. "Well, it still sucks."

When she didn't reply, he continued. "Anyways, now that we're getting to parts of the country where there is the potential for food, we need to be prepared that there are going to be many more of them than we saw out in the desert."

She relaxed slightly. The guy was doing his best to keep them all alive. "Hey, Jake, I don't fault you for getting with Carmen. You two seem great together."

"Thanks," he said, blushing.

Sidney bumped him with her shoulder. "So, when are we leaving?"

"We need to load the supplies we boxed up last night, but I was thinking we'd take off in a little less than an hour."

"Okay, good. That'll give me time to take a *tub* of baby wipes to the showers and clean up."

"Alright. Need me to do anything for you?"

She laughed. "Like what, scrub my back?" She shot him a playful smile. "Are you trying to start a harem?"

"What? No... I meant do you need me to—" His ears burned a bright red and his cheeks flushed, easily giving away his Irish heritage.

"No. Thank you. I'm fine, Jake."

Sidney turned and walked away, picking up a package of baby wipes as she passed them. She could feel Jake's eyes following her. The slight smile she'd had before turned into a full grin as she rounded the corner to the bathrooms.

She'd lived for so long without being able to trust anyone. Was the young soldier someone whom she could trust and allow inside of her defenses?

Maybe. She'd already thrown her lot in with them regarding her and her baby's life when they left Fort Bliss. However, the emotional scars from what she'd endured at the camp still ran deep. With time, and friendship, they would start to fade.

Until then, she'd remain cautiously optimistic that there were still good people in the world. She just had to find them.

"What the hell do you make of that, sir?" Sergeant Wyatt asked, pointing at the rusted red Ford truck swerving down the highway toward them.

"I don't know. Dickerson, pull over to the side of the road and drive forward slowly. Caitlyn, I need you to get on the fifty. Light 'em up if anything seems out of the ordinary."

"Out of the ordinary? You mean like the first person we've seen for a week is a drunk driver swerving all over the place kind of out of the ordinary or something else?"

Jake grimaced. "Come on. You know what I mean."

She dropped down inside the vehicle and slapped his boot. Over the intercom, she said, *"Just messing with you. I'm on it."*

Dickerson did as he'd ordered, pulling the Stryker over onto the shoulder of the road and then began creeping forward at what Jake guessed was about five miles an hour. When they were within fifty feet of the truck, Dickerson stopped, allowing the driver to swerve his way to them.

From up in the TC hatch, Jake saw that it was an old man in the driver's seat. His head kept falling forward and the truck would drift. Then he would snap his head back up and jerk the wheel, taking the truck back into the opposite lane. Jake waved his arms above his head and the truck stopped. He saw the old man's hands shift the vehicle into park and decided to hop down.

"Cover me," he said immediately before removing the combat vehicle crewman's helmet with the integrated headphones and slapping his regular Kevlar helmet into place. If Sergeant Wyatt said anything to him about not going, then he didn't hear her.

Jake raised the stock of his M-4 into his shoulder, but kept the barrel pointed toward the ground. "Let me see your hands!" he whispered harshly.

The old man raised them and then they disappeared into his lap. "Dammit," Jake cursed, advancing rapidly to the side of the truck.

"Are you bitten?"

The man shook his head. That's when Jake noticed the blood. "I said, did you get bitten by one of the infected?"

"No," the man croaked. "Shot. The girls. Help."

Jake debated with himself for only a moment. If this was a trap and it's where he was supposed to die, then he was prepared for it. The decision was already made in his mind. The man was obviously in some type of distress and he had to help him in any way that he could.

He stepped to the door and looked inside. There was blood around his midsection, the old tan Carhart jacket he wore was soaked through with it. "Fuck!" he grumbled. "What happened?"

"Girls. Help me…get them back."

Jake reached through the window. "Who did this?"

"Cullens. Those godless heathens." He coughed dryly, which Jake took to be a good sign. He wasn't a medic, and had only attended one combat lifesaver's course, but he knew that a wet cough could mean blood in the lungs and he'd need surgery, which they obviously couldn't do.

"I'm gonna open the door and look at your stomach, okay?"

He lifted his hand and then let it fall. Jake took that to mean that he was fine with being examined. "Are you sure you weren't bitten?"

"No, darn it," the man grunted in frustration. "Cullen boys shot me. Took the girls."

"Okay. We'll get to that in a minute," Jake assured him.

"Jake! Jake, what's going on?"

He turned to see the sergeant standing up on the vehicle. "He's been shot," Jake replied in a voice barely above normal talking range. He needed to be cognizant of the potential for infected in the area, but he hoped the fences along either side of the highway would act as a barrier in case any of them came from the overgrown fields. "Stomach wound. We need Carmen over here."

"Okay."

While his companions worked on unloading the Stryker, Jake turned back into the truck. He lifted the old man's shirt away from his belt line. A single, neat bullet hole was about two inches to the left of his navel. He'd taken biology in college, but couldn't remember if there were any vital organs in that area.

"I'm gonna look at your back. This will hurt like hell, okay?"

The man nodded, taking in a sharp breath as Jake leaned him forward. He lifted up the jacket and saw more blood. There was a small exit wound roughly on line with the entry wound. The hole leaked deep, maroon blood.

Again, Jake wracked his brain to remember his lifesaving classes. If it were a bright red color, that would mean arterial bleeding, which was infinitely worse, but was dark red blood as bad?

"What have you got?" Carmen asked from behind him. He saw that she'd brought the backboard that had been strapped to the side of the Stryker and the medical backpack.

"I think we need to get him out of the truck and bandage him up. Then we've gotta get off this road and into a building."

"Not what I asked you, Jake," she chastised him. "What have you got?"

He knew what she was asking. She wanted to know if it was worth using their precious medical supplies if the man was already a goner. "He has an entry wound about two inches to the left of his belly button and a clean exit wound on the back, roughly in line with the entry wound."

"Is he still bleeding?"

"Yeah."

"Color?"

"It's like a maroon. Seems to be coming out very slowly."

Carmen nodded. "Okay, that's all good. Let's get him out of the truck and strip his clothes off."

The older man helped the two of them immensely by sliding the best he could along the bench seat and holding tightly to the steering wheel as they maneuvered to lift him down from the cab.

Carmen opened the large medic backpack that Sergeant Wyatt had procured from somewhere and pulled out a package of QuikClot combat gauze. She'd examined and rearranged the pack to her liking over the past few days, presumably for moments like this when she needed to work fast.

Jake helped to roll the patient over as she bandaged the back wound first, and then the front. "I don't think it hit anything except intestines," she mumbled, tying the bandage. "There aren't any vital organs or bones where he was shot, so he was lucky in that regard. If his intestines are perforated, it's a 50-50 if he'll live. Intestinal leakage could cause infection. His body may fight it off or he could die from it."

"Is there anything you can do about it? I mean, like sew up his intestines if they did get hit?"

"I'm not a surgeon, Jake. I would do more damage than I would help—that's a guarantee. The best thing we can do for him is give him pain meds and antibiotics, then hope his body is strong enough to overcome this."

An iron-like hand clamped onto Jake's wrist, causing him to jump. "I need to get the girls," the older man said through gritted teeth, surprisingly clear.

"What girls?" Jake asked.

"Granddaughters. Cullens kidnapped them. Ambushed us." The hand on his wrist relaxed and

Jake thought he'd passed out, then the pressure returned. "Killed my friends."

"This— What do you mean they kidnapped them?"

"Are you stupid or something?" the man hissed. "Kidnapped them. You let your mind finish the rest. I need to rescue them."

"You're not going anywhere, sir," Carmen cut in. "You're lucky that you didn't bleed out and die from that injury. You've got a long road ahead of you. If you're going to recover, you have to rest and stay off your feet. Let your body heal."

"But my girls..." His voice cracked and for the first time, the old man's tough exterior fell away as tears streamed from the corner of his eyes. "I failed them, Sarah. I'm so sorry."

"Who's Sarah?"

The old man tried to sit up once again. "I have to rescue those girls."

"Hit him with some morphine," Jake ordered. As Carmen prepped the drug, he asked, "Mister. What's your name?"

"Vern."

"Okay, Vern. I need you to tell me where your hideout is. We'll take you back there and figure out what to do."

"Hideout? My farm is just up the road. Off B Highway." He pointed to the north. "But my girls are that way, near Tyrone. We gotta…" He slowly faded to sleep as the drugs hit him.

"Okay, let's load him up. I'll check the map, see if we can find this B Highway. He couldn't have gotten far driving like that, so we must be close."

"Are you gonna do anything about those kidnapped girls?" Carmen asked.

"I don't know yet. I sure as hell ain't gonna walk into an ambush with you and the kids in the back of the Stryker. We need to find a safe place to stay and sort this out. If his farm has been safe enough for the last seven months, then that's probably our best bet for a safe house while we figure out what we're doing."

Carmen nodded her head as she checked Vern's vitals. "Okay. He's still alive for right now. We need to get him someplace where he can rest. We might even have to use the blood transfusion kit. Won't know until I can get a real good look at him."

Jake grunted as he picked up one side of the litter and then set it back down. "What's up?" Carmen asked, setting her own end down.

"I just had an idea," he replied, jogging around to the side of the truck. He opened the glovebox and removed a stack of papers. Inside was the vehicle registration with an address on Zielne Road.

He held it up. "Got the address. I'll plug it into the GPS and see if we get a hit."

"Good thinking," she murmured as they picked up the litter again.

It'd be a long shot if the old man lived, but for some reason, Jake thought he would be just fine.

21

NEAR LIBERAL, KANSAS
OCTOBER 29TH

"Take it easy now, Vern," the Hispanic female cautioned. "You have a very serious injury that could end up killing you if you don't take some time off and rest."

"Don't care," he grunted, trying to sit up against one of the male soldier's restraining hands. He cried out in pain as his punctured abdominal muscles flexed. He relaxed and lay back against the pillows. "Holy smokes! That hurts something awful."

"I told you," she chastised him. "You need to rest."

"I sure do appreciate everything you folks have done for me, but what I need to do is rescue my granddaughters."

"We've been talking about that," the other male said. He wore body armor with a dusty first lieutenant's bar affixed to it.

"You in charge?" Vern asked, vaguely remembering that this guy was the one who came to help him at the truck.

"Kind of. It's... It's complicated."

"Complicated my behind, son," Vern grumbled. "You're either in charge or you ain't. Are you the highest ranking officer in your group?"

"Yes, but we aren't here on official military orders."

Vern huffed. "I been reading that the Army'd gone soft. Back in my day, the Army ran like a well-oiled machine and a soldier knew that his place was as a cog in that giant wheel. And you can bet we knew who was in charge at any given time."

"You were in the Army?" the lieutenant asked.

"Seven years. Vietnam for three of 'em, then I wised up and left the service."

"Wow. Thank you for—"

"Can it, son. I don't need no thanks. I *need* to get up and go find my girls." He gestured angrily at the big soldier standing above him. "Now either you tell Mongo here to let me up, *Lieutenant*, or you go get that sergeant to tell him to."

"Sir, give me a chance to talk here. My name is Jake Murphy, this is Private Dickerson, and this," he rubbed the Hispanic woman's shoulders, "is Carmen Agusto. She's a nurse."

"Hi," the woman said with a genuinely warm smile.

Vern nodded but didn't say anything. "We also have Sergeant Wyatt. The other woman in our group is Sidney Bannister. And there's Carmen's two kids."

"Where's the rest of your unit? The Internet said the government was organizing a response force."

"Ah, well… They were overrun. We're all that's left."

Vern whistled low. "That ain't good. Just the—what—five of you? That's all?"

"I'm sure that more got out, Mr. Campbell," the lieutenant stated. "We just don't know."

He grunted. "Ok, so just the five adults. It's nice to meet you and all that, but I need—"

"Sir, please," Lieutenant Murphy said. "Let me finish."

"Then quit beatin' around the bush and get to your point."

The officer frowned. "You lost several men in the fight—we saw their bodies. This place is too much for you to maintain on your own."

"I can manage."

"Okay, look," he said, appearing to finally be getting to the point. "We're looking to find a long-term place to stay. You can't get up and your granddaughters have been kidnapped. We want to help you rescue them."

"In exchange for staying here on my farm," Vern surmised.

The officer looked across the room to where the female soldier leaned against a dresser. Vern tried to look over quick enough to discern what their silent communication meant, but he missed it. By the time he was looking at the woman, her face was a blank slate, staring back at him.

"Yeah. We'd like to stay—only through winter. And then we'll be moving on."

Vern tried to sit up again, but the white fire in his gut made him reconsider. "Fine. You help me get my girls back and the lot of you can stay through winter. No free chicken, though. You'll have to work."

"We wouldn't have it any other way, sir."

He started to say something about how deserters couldn't be trusted, but decided to hold his tongue.

These people were his best bet at getting Sally and Katie back from those monsters. "Alright, what do you need from me?"

"Information," Lieutenant Murphy replied. "Tell us everything you know about these Cullen brothers."

22

NEAR TYRONE, OKLAHOMA
OCTOBER 29TH

Sally's vision swam from the blow. She'd tried to stop Russ from strapping Katie to the bed and been rewarded with a vicious backhand across her cheekbone.

"Hey, now, little brother," Tim chided. "Don't damage the merchandise."

"Merchandise? We ain't sellin' 'em," the fatter of the two men said.

"It's a goddamned figure of speech, Russ! Dammit if your mother didn't raise the dumbest son of a bitch in the county."

"Yeah, she had you," Russ giggled, obviously amused at his own joke. "I stood watch while you went at that old broad for forty-five minutes. It's my turn, you selfish bastard."

Sally heard a grunt as Tim must have punched his younger brother. "Damn you. When I tell you that we gotta keep this one alive, I mean it." There was a dull *thumping* sound of fists against skin.

She used her bound hands to wipe away the tears, snot, and blood on her face, risking a glance at the two men. They were really going at it. Both of them seemingly equally matched as they traded punch for punch. Russ was already stripped down to just his underwear and the impact of his brother's punches made his fat ripple with each one.

"I'm so sick of you telling me what to do!" Russ shouted, oblivious to the fact that loud noises brought the infected.

"I'm the only reason you're still alive, you dumb motherfucker."

Sally saw the nude form of Katie on the bed. Both of her hands were tied to the bedposts and it looked like one of her ankles. The other was free, and she was using it as leverage to try to push herself away from the Cullen brothers.

"I hate you!" Russ screamed, kicking Tim hard in the crotch.

Tim doubled over in pain, but managed to catch Russ' foot between his legs. He reached out and grabbed the testicles of his younger brother through the underwear.

"*Aiyeee!*" Russ screamed as Tim's massive paw squeezed his testicles.

The two of them tumbled over in a heap, Russ twisting to get away from Tim's grip. "You little fuckstain," Tim hissed. "I've had it with you. I'm gonna gut you like a fucking fish and keep all three of these women for myself."

Three? Sally's mind reeled in confusion. She hadn't seen another woman in the room. When she'd woken up, her and Katie were tied up with duct tape on the floor. Who was the other — *Momma!*

Her mother had stayed in the house when everyone went out to fight the infected. If they'd gotten Katie off the lookout perch, then it made sense that they could have gotten her as well.

She wormed her way along the floor as best she could with hands and feet bound. The two men seemed intent on beating the life from one another and she had every intention of getting her and her sister out of there. The floor was nasty, covered in what looked like bloodstains and dried, flaky white circles of— *Oh God*. She suppressed her revulsion at the evidence of what these two had been using this room for and continued crawling. She had to make it.

A noise by the door drew her attention. It was a rapid, electronic tapping sound. She knew she'd heard it before, but couldn't quite place it in her current state.

One of the brothers screamed and grunted simultaneously as the tapping sound continued. Russ had pulled an electronic Taser from somewhere and was applying it to Tim's neck.

Sally brought her knees to her chest and began to rapidly unwind the tape around her ankles. She kept glancing at the brothers. Russ now lay on his side, facing away from her with his hands between his legs, moaning hoarsely in pain. Tim appeared to be unconscious.

She finished unwrapping her legs and tried momentarily to free her hands, but it was still no use. There was no way to undo the tape around her wrists without using her fingers. With nothing else to do, she stood and rushed over to where Katie was taped down to the bed.

Her younger sister's eyes went wide in recognition, but she wisely kept her mouth shut. On the floor, the men were beginning to stir. Sally looked for a weapon of any kind. Nothing. There was nothing in this room besides the bed.

Sally reached out and began to unravel the tape on Katie's ankle. Russ sat up in her periphery vision. "Hey!" he said, trying to get up.

His bulk worked against him, and he had to put his hand down to push himself up. That's when Tim grabbed his arm and jerked it violently from under him. "Fucking motherfucker," Tim snarled as he worked his way into a standing position.

"Tim, no!"

Tim pulled his leg back and kicked Russ violently in the ribs. Sally wasn't sure, but she thought she heard some of them break. "I'll teach you to tase me, you fat fuck." He kicked his brother again, causing Russ to wrap around his foot.

The Taser slid out of Russ' grip across the floor to where Sally stood, petrified. If she was going to survive this ordeal, then she had to push past her fear. Her family needed her. She bent down and picked up the Taser.

"Now what do you think *you're* doing?" the older Cullen asked, turning to face her.

"I'm going to take my sister—and my mother—and leave."

"Oh, is that right?" Tim sneered.

Sally held the Taser in front of her like a shield. "Yeah, that's right." She'd tried, and failed, to add steel to her voice. As she talked, her fingers tapped against the buttons on the side of the device and she squeezed them, trying to determine how it worked. Depressing both buttons at the same time sent a small blue arc of electricity between the two prongs along with the stuttering tap sound she'd heard earlier.

"You're gonna put that little toy down, missy." He took a menacing step toward her and then yelped in pain as Russ bit into his calf muscle through his jeans.

Tim turned to kick at Russ and Sally slid up to the headboard. She had to set the Taser down to unwrap the tape around Katie's wrists.

"You little—"

"Look out!" Katie screamed.

Sally picked up the Taser and pushed the buttons just as Tim lunged at her. The prongs hit him in the face, one in his eye and the other along his temple. He dropped instantly, knocked out cold from the electricity.

"I didn't want to," Russ whimpered, holding his ribs as he scooted backward toward the door. He had blood oozing from a cut on his forehead and his broken nose. "We tried to—"

Sally leapt over Tim's unconscious form and zapped Russ in his outstretched hands. He screamed, his body flinging backward as his spine went rigid. The back of his head impacted against the hard wooden floors, knocking him out as well.

She walked back across the room, tasing Tim in the face when she walked by. "We need to get out of here," she stated, setting the Taser down to finish unwrapping Katie's hands.

"Where are we gonna go?" the younger girl asked.

"Anywhere but here. They have Mom too."

Katie nodded. "I heard her screams earlier. I think she's upstairs."

Sally helped her sister to her feet and then picked up her clothes, handing them to her. "Hallway," she said, pointing at the door.

When they got into the hallway, she turned and closed the bedroom door. There was a deadbolt on the *outside* of the door, which she twisted home. "That won't hold them long. We need to get Mom and go."

Katie wiggled into her blue jeans and nodded enthusiastically. "Weapons. We need weapons."

They wasted precious seconds looking in the foyer for anything of use. Again, they came up empty. The kitchen lay off to the side and Sally went over to the counter. An empty knife block rested under a disgusting microwave. She searched the counter, shoving used plates and dirty cups out of the way until she noticed the sink. *There!* Two knives sat on the edge of the sink, apparently ready to be used—again.

She snatched them both up and went into the foyer. "Any luck?" she asked.

"No. I don't know where they put those guns."

Sally handed her a knife. "No time. Here, cut the tape on my wrists. I can't do it."

Katie sawed on the tape for a moment before cursing from the bedroom startled her, causing the knife to tumble to the floor. She cried out in fear and frustration.

"Katie, look at me," Sally said calmly. "We're in charge here. We have the power. Focus on what you're doing."

The younger Campbell nodded and bent to retrieve the knife. The bedroom door handle shook violently for a moment and then one of the men began to pound on it, yelling obscenities.

"Go upstairs and get Mom," Sally directed. "I'll stay here and deal with them if they get out."

Katie nodded and scampered up the stairs.

"I'm gonna cut you into little pieces, girlie," Tim roared, trying the handle again. "All your people are dead. You can't get away from me."

There was a sharp snap as the handle broke from his efforts on the other side. The cheap metal knob fell onto the foyer floor. "There you are," Tim said, his eye appearing in the vacant space where the handle had been. "I'm gonna enjoy— *Hey!*"

She jabbed the end of the knife through the opening, hoping to stab him through the eye. No such luck.

"You're not gonna do a damned thing to me or my family ever again, asshole," she hissed, this time the hard edge in her voice came naturally.

"Oh, don't worry. You haven't seen the last of me, you little cu—"

"Sally! I need help," Katie called from the top of the stairs. "I found Mom, but she's pretty beat up. I was able to get her to the stairs. I can't get her down without dropping her."

Sally eyed the door for a moment, thrust the blade through the hole once again to warn Tim off, and then rushed up the stairs.

Her mother was bruised and bloodied. The shirt she'd worn that morning had most of the buttons missing and her chest was exposed, revealing fingernail scrapes, bite marks, and what looked like cigarette burns.

"Oh, God. Momma!"

The older woman stared vacantly ahead, and Sally wasn't sure if she even knew where she was. Katie leaned toward her to add as much space between their mother and her mouth. "They tore her up pretty bad," she said. "There's blood all over…down there. I think…" Her voice trailed off.

Sally nodded hard, then ducked under her mother's arm. Between the two girls, they got her down the stairs. They set her down on the bench so they could begin putting her shoes on.

"Jeff!" her mother shouted hysterically. "I didn't want to, Jeff. They made me!"

The sudden shouts of confession from her mother almost made Sally drop her knife. "Stop it, Mom. You didn't ask for that to happen."

"Oh yes she did," Tim's voice lilted through the hole. "In fact, she begged for more. Even when I used that baseball bat of yours, I couldn't fill her up enough to satisfy her desires. She's a hellcat, that one right there. That's why I took her first. Don't worry, sweetheart. You're next."

Sally blanched. The fact that her baseball bat had been used to assault her mother made the act even more heinous.

"No! Jeff, I promise you," her mother shouted.

"Mom! Dad's dead," Sally grunted, shoving her mother's boot into place. "He's been dead for months. I need you to—"

"*No!*" her mother shrieked. "He's not dead, you lying harlot. He's waiting for me. Waiting for me outside!"

She pushed Sally roughly, causing her to fall hard onto her butt. Tim's laughter rang in her ears as her mother limped to the door. "I wouldn't do that, baby," he half-sang through the hole.

If Katherine Campbell heard him—or if she had the mental capacity to understand him—she didn't acknowledge the elder Cullen brother. She threw open the front door and was immediately set upon by several of the infected that had been on the porch. She screamed in agony as they tore at her flesh.

"She's gone," Sally howled and snatched Katie's wrist. She pulled her away from their mother toward the back of the house.

"I told her not to do that!" Tim yelled gleefully after them.

The girls fled to the interior of the home, searching for a way out. The screams of the infected chasing after them added to their panic.

"Back door!" Katie breathed heavily, pointing at a barred door that led outside from the living room.

They rushed to it. There was no time to worry whether there were infected on the other side of the door. There were *definitely* infected inside the house. They had to take their chances outside. She twisted the handle and flung the door wide, tensing in case she was assaulted by teeth and ragged fingernails.

They never came. She opened her eyes. The way was clear.

"Go! Go!" Sally shouted to Katie, shoving her in front of her and causing her to stumble down the three or four wooden steps to the ground.

She turned around, grasping the door handle and pulled it closed. The screams of the infected reverberated through the house and a hand shot into the space between the door and the frame, stopping the door from closing all the way.

Sally pulled hard on the door, but the creature pulled against her, practically pulling her off her feet as she clung to the handle. "Damn you!" she cursed at the infected, stabbing ineffectively against its hands and arms through the open space in the doorway.

The infected screamed back at her. It wanted to kill her, to turn her. Sally wasn't ready to give up her life so easily. She thrust the kitchen knife toward its face, the blade bouncing off teeth and into the soft flesh at the back of the crazed beast's throat.

It gagged, letting go of the door to slap uselessly at the knife handle protruding from its mouth. Sally used the split second to her advantage, yanking the door closed.

"Sally! Did you get—Are you?"

"I'm fine!" she yelled. "I lost my knife though."

"I still have mine," Katie assured her. "This way!"

Sally stumbled down the stairs. It was either dusk or dawn; she wasn't sure which. There was enough light to see that a barbed wire fence lined either side of the path they found themselves on. The fences ran all the way from the house to the barn, giving the Cullens a safe route between the two.

They raced to the barn and went through the doorway. The interior held an assortment of the standard farm tools, but it also acted as a garage. There was a Jeep and two old pickup trucks inside.

The girls searched both quickly, coming up with zero sets of keys.

"That door isn't going to keep Tim and Russ locked up forever," Sally said in frustration. "And I doubt that even all of those infected will be any trouble for them. They must have planned for something like that to happen, that's why they allowed them to be outside their front door."

Sally set her jaw, kicking the discarded straw on the floor in anger. "We have to leave on foot," she decided.

Katie stared, wide-eyed at her for a moment and then accepted the decision. "There are some farm tools over by the other door that we can use as weapons."

Sally hugged her little sister as they grabbed an axe and a shovel, both with dried blood along their edges. They'd been used for self-defense before.

They opened the door to the outside cautiously, peering through the crack to see if they would be able to make it without a horde of infected spotting them immediately. The shifting of several bodies startled Sally and she slammed the door shut.

After a moment, there was no pounding on the side of the barn to indicate that they'd been seen, so

Sally eased the door open again. Once more, bodies shifted in front of her, but they didn't advance.

Allowing her eyes to adjust to the deepening gloom of the night outside, she saw that there were several infected trapped inside a cattle trailer. They banged against the sides, but their broken, twisted fingers couldn't grasp the metal crossbeams.

The realization of what she saw dawned on her. "Son of a bitch," she murmured, waving Katie out the door.

"What is it?"

"These are the same infected that were at the farm. See how their fingers are all broken, and…" She stepped close to examine one of them. "Yeah, they don't have any teeth. Probably don't have tongues either. That's why they aren't screaming and alerting the others."

There were several loud gunshots from inside the house and Sally accidently allowed a squeal of shock to escape her lips. Two more gunshots rang out and then the back door of the house banged open.

"I'll find you little bitches!" Tim shouted into the night. "When I do, you'll regret everything about tonight. You hear me! I'm going to make you *wish* you'd stayed with us the first time around."

He bellowed in frustration and fired a pistol into the air four times. "I'm coming for you!"

Sally and Katie slipped into the overgrown cornfield behind the barn. They had no idea which way they were headed. They only knew that they needed to put as much distance between them and that lunatic at the farmhouse as they could.

23

NEAR TYRONE, OKLAHOMA
OCTOBER 29TH

"There's thermal activity inside and out of the farmhouse," Caitlyn said into her helmet microphone. She leaned back away from the TWS display and gripped the .50 cal's joystick. With a few deft movements, perfected over hundreds of hours as a gunner, she guided the target reticle pattern on the mob of infected around the front door.

"What are the ones outside doing?" Lieutenant Murphy asked. His voice sounded tinny and distant through the helmet speakers.

"Just milling about as far as I can tell. Something inside has them all agitated."

"Probably the girls' screams."

"Ugh," she groaned, not wanting to think about what they could potentially be walking into at the house. The old man said the two men had been deranged perverts *before* the outbreak. There was no telling how far they'd gone without the threat of law enforcement officers discovering what they were doing.

"Okay, I'm gonna start clearing the infected, just like we discussed."

Caitlyn didn't answer. There was some kind of ruckus going on in the room to the left of the first floor hallway. Her thermal imaging was good, but not good enough to tell her what was really going on inside the home. However, the infected outside were lit up like Christmas trees.

"Hold on. Something's happening inside," Caitlyn cautioned. "Two large heat signatures—those could be the Cullens—seem to be embracing, or… No. They're fighting."

"Fighting? Anyone else in the room with them?"

"I can't tell through the mass of infected out front," she replied. She continued to observe for a moment and then said, "Two smaller forms have emerged into the hallway. The two larger ones are still inside the room."

"Son of a bitch," the lieutenant breathed. *"Those girls may end up doing the job for us."*

"Yeah… One of the larger forms is at the door. Looks like he's banging on the door from the *inside*."

"That's my cue then," he said. Above her, Caitlyn could hear the muffled sound of the suppressed M-2010 sniper rifle firing and then the soft *chink* of the brass cartridge falling onto the Stryker's roof when Jake cycled a new round.

One of the shapes went up the stairs and then reappeared with another. Caitlyn had no way of knowing whether the heat signatures she saw were from friendlies or hostiles. Another shape ran up the stairs and all three of them came down toward the first floor.

"I'm willing to be that those are the girls. Looks like they have Mrs. Campbell," Caitlyn surmised.

"Good. I'm knocking out the infected slow and steady up here," Murphy grunted. *"Hold on!"*

"I see it," she answered. Some moron had opened the front door. The remaining infected grabbed the person in the doorway and bright sprays of blood that quickly faded spurted skyward. "Son of a bitch."

"They're in the house," the lieutenant stated. *"I repeat: the infected are in the house."*

"Well, that's that, then." She leaned back. If the infected were inside, then the girls were as good as gone. She tapped the joystick back and forth, then zoomed in with the camera. There was nothing to see… "Hold up. There's—"

Gunfire rang out clearly in the early night. "Somebody is shooting inside the house."

"I can see the flashes through the windows," he replied.

"I'll find you little bitches!" someone yelled from the back of the house, followed by several shots. Caitlyn didn't know where the person was shooting, but any bullet headed downrange was bad in her opinion.

"I'm going in," Murphy announced. *"I can't stand by while those lunatics are shooting at a couple of innocent women."*

"Jake! I mean, sir, what are you—" The lieutenant's CVC helmet dropped inside the crew compartment, followed by the M-2010.

He grabbed his M-4 and helmet, then looked at Caitlyn. "I need you to cover me. Got it?"

"Yeah, I got it." Then he was gone.

"I'm going too," Eric said over the helmet speakers.

"Eric! No, what are you doing?" she muttered, unable to determine if the big dummy had heard her.

She saw his head appear in the lower left corner of the gun camera as he trotted after the lieutenant. "Son of a bitch."

In her monitor, Caitlyn could see flashes of light from the house. Jake and Eric fired back. They were in a firefight with the people inside.

She had no way of knowing who was shooting, but she knew that those girls they were sent here to rescue wouldn't be firing on them. She took that logic as an authorization to go weapons hot.

Zooming the reticle pattern in on a window in the front of the house, she waited until there was another flash of gunfire, then she feathered the trigger, sending twenty or thirty rounds screaming from the .50 mounted on top of the Stryker into the defender. The bullets tore through the old clapboard siding and she saw the heat signature stagger backward, then fall down. She watched for a moment longer to see if she'd put an end to that threat. The person she'd shot did not get back up.

With that threat neutralized, Caitlyn scanned back and forth along the house, but there were no more muzzle flashes. If there was more than one person shooting from the house, they were probably holding their fire because of the machine gun. She pulled the camera back for a wider angle and saw one of her teammates stand up, waving an arm. By the size of him, she thought it might be Eric.

Then a flash of light came from one of the upper windows. Without hesitation, she slewed the machine gun upward and peppered the house, noticing that the heat signature was no longer at the window.

"Goddamn. Fucker's good," she muttered aloud to herself. She scanned the entire area again with the same result: no one was there. She wondered if she'd got him. Confident that she'd neutralized the threat on the second floor, she zoomed the camera out once more and noticed a large blob of orange, red, and white. One of her friends knelt over the other one. The one on the ground had several dark patches of blue, meaning he'd been shot and the fluid was rapidly cooling in the night air.

"Oh, goddamn it!" she yelled, pulling herself up through the gunners hatch to the roof of the Stryker. She skittered and skid along the surface until she made her way to the ground.

Caitlyn ran at a full sprint. If Eric was hurt, she'd never forgive herself for agreeing that he should come on this stupid rescue mission. She didn't care that the lieutenant had told her to cover the house until he signaled the all clear. The only thing that mattered to her was getting to Eric. They'd talked about their future. Planned to have children one day after this was all over. *If he...*

"Eric!" she shouted as she ran toward the downed man, careless of noise discipline. "Eric, I'm coming for—"

Jake returned fire at the house, unsure of where the initial round had come from. It had impacted in the gravel only a few inches to his right. He juked to the left and fired another burst in the general direction of the house.

"On your six, sir!"

He looked back in time to see Private Dickerson running up behind him. Together they fired their unsuppressed M-4s, heedless of the noise that was sure to bring any infected in the area. The blossoms of fire from the end of Dickerson's weapon stung Jake's eyes with every shot. More rounds came speeding their way from the house and they both fell into the prone.

Jake searched for any type of cover, but they were in the middle of a driveway. Dickerson fired again and stood, sprinting a few meters before he used his rifle to get down and return fire at the house.

The lieutenant shook his head. Private Dickerson hadn't been out of Basic Training that long when all of this hit and the old three-to-five second rush technique was one of the primary things they taught recruits. "Fuck it," he muttered, then shouted, "Cover me while I move!"

"Got you covered!" Dickerson squeezed off a few more rounds.

As Jake stood and began sprinting, the .50 cal on the Stryker opened up behind him. He dove for the ground instinctively before looking up. On the right side of the farmhouse, window glass tinkled as it fell to the gravel. The wooden siding around the first floor window was covered with bullet holes. Muffled gasps of pain emanated from inside the house.

"She got him!" Dickerson laughed, standing up. "That's my girl. Damn, sir. You see that shooting, sir?"

"Dickerson! Get—" A single shot cut him off as Dickerson crumpled to the ground. "Son of a bitch!"

Sergeant Wyatt unleashed another sustained volley from the .50, this time focusing on a second story window. Glass shattered and the old wood splintered. He waited for several seconds to see if there'd be a response from the shooter, but there was none. She must have gotten that one too.

Two Cullen brothers, two shooters down.

Jake ran at a low crouch to help Private Dickerson. The man lay face down on the gravel and he flipped him over. Blood covered his chest. He hadn't been wearing body armor because he couldn't fit in the driver's hatch with it on, so there was nothing to stop the rounds from tearing into him.

He checked the man's pulse. He wasn't breathing. Jake tried desperately to remember the combat lifesaving skills he'd been taught. Then it came to him. The first thing he needed to do was check for breathing. Without oxygen, nothing else mattered.

Dickerson wasn't breathing. He positioned himself up over the top of the private and blew two quick breaths into his mouth.

"Eric!" Sergeant Wyatt shouted. Jake glanced at the Stryker as he pressed down on the man's chest. She was running full sprint toward them. She'd abandoned the .50 cal.

"Eric," she yelled again. "I'm coming for—"

Another blast came from the house and Jake threw himself to the ground, grabbing his rifle. He fired three quick rounds in the direction of the house.

"Oh god!" Wyatt screamed. "Medic!"

Jake grimaced. This mission wasn't going the way he'd envisioned it. The girls had somehow gotten away during a break in by a group of infected and now both members of his team were down, one permanently.

"Fuck!" he shouted in frustration. He instinctively wanted to go help Wyatt, but he since he had no idea where the sniper was, he knew that going back to the wounded soldier would put him in in the gunman's line of sight for sure.

He had to move or he would be the sniper's next target. Using the butt of his rifle, Jake surged to his feet. The Stryker was over a hundred yards away, so he sprinted toward the closest cover available.

Jake slammed his shoulder into the half-open farmhouse door, tumbling inside.

24

NEAR TYRONE, OKLAHOMA
OCTOBER 29TH

Jake pushed himself away from the bloody body of a middle-aged woman. Her eyes were open, but the gaping hole in her throat told him that she'd never transition into one of the infected. She was dead.

On his feet once again, he flipped down the night vision monocle mounted to his helmet, bathing the room in a green glow in half of his vision. Jake slapped at the light switch, plunging the small foyer into darkness in an attempt to give himself a small advantage over the shooter who already knew the layout of the home. He had no way of knowing where that sniper was, whether he was in the house or in the barn. Jake would have to clear the house before he could attempt any type of exfil or first aid for Sergeant Wyatt.

He couldn't remember how many rounds he'd fired so he dropped the magazine and slammed a new one home quickly. He bent and retrieved it, realizing he'd been very low on ammo before the mag change.

There was a bedroom immediately off the foyer. Inside, a large man in only his underwear lay dead, perforated by a half-dozen of the .50 cal rounds. It wasn't a pretty sight, even with the washed out green color of his night vision.

He closed the door quietly behind himself and slid across the foyer to the kitchen. It didn't take long to see that it was clear. Several steps toward the back of the house and he stood behind the doorframe leading into the living room. On first glance it was clear, but he had to enter the room and clear the area behind the couch where he couldn't see.

First floor clear, he told himself as he slinked toward the staircase in the foyer. Assaulting up a set of stairs was infinitely more dangerous than defending them from above, a fact that he was acutely aware of as he placed a foot on the first creaky step.

The first of several screams reached his ears as he eased his weight from the floor onto the stairs. The infected from the surrounding area were being drawn toward the sound of the gunfire—not the least of which was the .50 cal that Sergeant Wyatt fired earlier. He checked behind himself, quickly verifying that he'd latched the front door. It looked secure.

The infected outside would absolutely be a problem. *For later*, he told himself. He had to find the sniper before he could worry about them.

He turned back then crept slowly upward. Jake heard the heavy breathing before he'd gone more than three steps. He paused, waiting for a moment to try to identify where the sounds were coming from. It was muted, and not entirely clear, so he didn't think the shooter was on the landing, prepared to shoot him in the face the moment his head appeared.

Jake wished he had a flash-bang that he could use to stun the gunman, but of course, he didn't have anything like that. He listened for a few more seconds, then rushed up the stairs. To his left, a hole appeared in the plaster as the sounds of gunfire reverberated through the upstairs hallway.

Jake dove to the right through the haze of disturbed plaster dust, catching his hipbone on the banister post. The pain was jarring, but would pale in comparison to getting shot, so he ignored it, scrambling away from what he assumed to be a bedroom.

Jake flipped over onto his stomach and aimed his rifle at the doorway. Muffled curses drifted from the room and he could hear the clicking of metal as the gunman tried to clear a misfeed.

Jake surged to his feet, rushing across the small hallway. In seconds, he was at the doorway and saw the shape of a large man fumbling with a rifle. He fired two quick shots before he swept his back against the wall outside. One of the rounds might have hit the gunman, but he didn't think the other one found home.

The shooter fired one more shot and the rifle misfired again. Jake turned the corner, lifting his weapon. He squeezed off two more rounds, both finding their mark. The man shuddered and the rifle fell away.

He aimed and shot the man through the top of his head—this world was no place for mercy or for taking chances. He checked the closet, and then cleared the rest of the upstairs before returning to the bedroom where he'd killed the man he assumed to be the sniper.

His legs were a shredded mess. The Stryker's .50 cal had blasted a hole in one thigh and almost severed his other leg below the knee. Jake tried to piece together the sequence of events. The man's weapon, a bolt-action 30-06 hunting rifle, had some shrapnel damage to the receiver, likely from the .50 and was the cause of the jam that saved his life. A pistol lay on the opposite side of the bed. The slide was locked back. Empty.

The sniper, one of the Cullen brothers he assumed, had still been able to shoot at Sergeant Wyatt after he'd been shot, proving that he was a determined asshole. Most people would have given up in that situation.

"Shit!" Jake groaned. Caitlyn was injured outside with all those infected inbound.

He leapt down the stairs and went into the room where the other brother died. Through the broken window, he could see a couple of the creatures milling about on the gravel between the house and the Stryker. Wyatt was nowhere to be seen.

He took his time, aiming carefully for headshots on the infected. While they would certainly die of their wounds in a few hours if he hit them elsewhere, a headshot was the only guaranteed way to put them down instantly.

In minutes, it was over. All the infected in the immediate area were dead. Jake switched magazines once again and stuck his head out the window to make sure the front porch was clear. It was, so he pulled himself back through, careful to avoid the jagged shards of glass. He went to the front door and left the house open behind him.

He jogged across the gravel toward the Stryker. Passing Private Dickerson's body, he said a silent prayer of thanks that it hadn't been desecrated. That would only last a few hours though. Once the body began to decompose and the infected were able to smell him, they would begin feeding.

He made it to the vehicle and found Sergeant Wyatt. She'd tried to get back into the Stryker, but likely couldn't reach the switch up high to open the ramp. Jake couldn't remember if they'd engaged the combat lock inside before they left Vern Campbell's farm, so it might have been a wasted effort on her part anyway.

"Wyatt, are you okay?"

Her head lolled sideways as she looked up at him. "Lucky... I didn't...shoot you," she gasped, blood oozing from the side of her mouth.

"No," he replied, smiling. "I'm gonna look you over, okay?"

She nodded and he positioned her onto her back. He pulled the quick release straps on her body armor and it fell away, revealing a dark stain across the t-shirt she wore underneath. A quick look under the shirt showed an entry wound near her clavicle. The sniper was up high, so the 7.62-millimeter round must have went through the open space between her neck and the armor. He was probably aiming for her head, but his own wounds threw off the shot.

"How... How bad?" She was shivering.

"Just a little hole," he lied. "I need to see your back, so I'm gonna roll you over, okay?"

She didn't answer. He rolled her toward him and saw a massive, bloody hole bigger than a softball near her kidney. The bullet traveled completely through her torso and exited down low. The body armor probably enhanced the damage since the kinetic energy of the round had nowhere to go when it left her body.

Under the best circumstances, her injury would have been critical. Here, in the middle of a cornfield, surrounded by the infected, with no medical personnel, it was an absolute death sentence.

She gurgled, trying to say something that he couldn't understand. Putting her on her side had filled her lung with blood. "Shit," he laid her back down on her back, allowing the blood to flow out of her body like it had been when he first arrived.

There was little he could do except make her last moments as peaceful as possible. "You did good, Caitlyn," he cooed, taking her head in his lap and stroking her hair. "You saved my life. You shot *both* of those Cullen brothers."

She blinked slowly, and opened her mouth, but no words came out. Caitlyn Wyatt died on his lap in the middle of fucking nowhere.

"Hurry!" Sally hissed. There'd been a terrible amount of gunfire from the farmhouse—including what sounded like a machine gun from a war movie. She could only assume that the Cullens were shooting at them. It was paramount that they put every bit of distance that they could between them and those two lunatics.

"I'm running…" Katie wheezed. "We…need to slow…down."

Sally turned, trying to see her sister in the failing light. The corn stalks were overgrown, easily seven feet tall and blocking out the new moon overhead. Through the shriveling ears of corn and dried leaves, she could see Katie holding a hand against her side. They'd only been running for a few minutes. If the brothers drove through the field in one of those trucks, they could catch up to them easily.

She slowed to a walk, letting Katie catch up to her. "We need to keep going. Are you okay?"

Katie nodded, taking great gulps of air as her chest heaved with exhaustion. "I just…just need a minute."

"We should slide over a couple of cornrows so we aren't as easy to track."

They did their best to slip between the dried out stalks of corn without breaking them or leaving clear evidence of their passing. Once they'd traversed six rows, and received multiple scrapes from the coarse leaves, Sally decided they'd gone far enough and began walking down the narrow space between rows again.

"Where are we going?" Katie asked.

Sally shrugged. "I don't know. Anywhere but here."

"Are we gonna go back to Grandpa's?"

Sally thought about it for a moment. "Probably. I mean, where else are we gonna go?"

"What if those two are waiting for us when we get there?"

"Then we'll sneak away. Maybe try our luck in Liberal or something."

That seemed to satisfy her sister's questions so they walked in silence for a few minutes. Then the telltale sounds of feet slapping against the ground and breaking corn stalks made them freeze. Katie's hand shot out and gripped Sally's upper arm as they both ducked down as quietly as they could.

Three rows away, several infected ran by, rushing toward the sound of gunfire at the farmhouse. The girls held their breath, fearing that even the slightest exhale would attract the creatures' attention. Katie's fingernails dug into the flesh on the underside of Sally's bicep, probably drawing blood. But neither of them dared to move.

At the farmhouse a quick flurry of gunshots caused the nearest infected to begin screaming as they ran, heedless of the stalks of corn tearing at them. After the infected had passed their hiding area, the night was quiet once more. *Are the Cullens shooting at each other, or are they shooting at the infected that'd answered the call of Tim's gun?*

They were questions that Sally couldn't answer, and to be honest, she didn't care if she ever learned the answer. She just never wanted to see the brothers again.

They stayed hidden, crouched low until Sally's knees began to ache. She eased down gently onto them, relieving the pressure from her quads. As she did that, Katie's fingernails eased out of her skin, which felt worse than when she was squeezing. The fire-like pain threatened to make her cry out, so she bit her knuckle.

There were still infected in the corn. Each time they thought the coast was clear another would stumble by. They stayed put for almost thirty minutes, enduring the prolonged feeling of being hunted. The minutes were interspersed with random gunfire, telling the girls that the Cullens were still out there, searching.

Finally, Katie whispered into her ear. "I think it's clear."

Sally agreed with her and they clasped hands, rising up. "We just need to keep going. I think we're headed toward the highway."

Katie squeezed her fingers in response and they stepped off, only to stop dead in their tracks. Behind them, someone was coming *toward* their position. They could hear the muffled curses as stalks of corn snapped, echoing across the night. The use of words meant it was not one of the infected.

"Give me the knife," Sally directed. She was done being the victim. She was going to make those assholes pay.

Her sister complied, passing the knife into her hand. A corn stalk broke close by, seemingly right behind them. It was dark down in between the rows of corn. A wide shape materialized in the darkness.

Sally lunged with the knife, aiming for her pursuer's chest.

25

NEAR TYRONE, OKLAHOMA
OCTOBER 29TH

Jake gasped in surprise, stumbling backward after he took a hard hit to his chest. He caught himself before he fell and made even more noise than he already had pursuing the girls through the cornfield. He looked down at his body, the night vision monocular he wore showed him something he never imagined possible.

"What the—" A large kitchen knife was embedded into the Kevlar lining of his ballistic armor. It dangled impotently from the fabric, having hit the ceramic armor plate underneath and not gone any farther.

Movement directly in front of him made him throw his arm up as a fist came out of his blind side and hit him squarely across the jaw. Night vision devices were great for things directly in front of the wearer, but they effectively rendered them blind to everything else.

Jake had endured the required boxing matches at West Point like every cadet before him, so he was familiar with getting punched. The blow was hard and the bare knuckles slamming into his jaw made his eyes water, but it wasn't as strong as an average male's punch.

"*Stop!*" he whispered, tensing for another blow from the woman who'd evaded his sight. "Your grandfather sent me to rescue you."

"What?"

"*Shhh!* Keep your voice down."

A woman appeared in front of him. In the green glare, he couldn't really discern any of her features, but it *had* to be one of the Campbell girls. The odds were too astronomically great that there'd be another survivor in the field just then.

"My grandfather is dead," she whispered.

"No. He survived. We found him out near the highway. He's been shot up pretty bad, but he should pull through."

The woman turned and he looked beyond her to where another girl eased up cautiously. They gripped hands and the first one asked, "Who are you?"

"Jake Murphy, from the US Army," he replied with a smile that she probably couldn't see in the darkness.

Her hand flew to her mouth. "Grandpa was right. The Army is here to save us!"

Jake's smile faltered. "Not exactly... We're not safe out here. We need to get to the safety of a building."

"What about Tim and Russ?"

"Are those the Cullens? The ones who kidnapped you?"

"Yeah."

"Dead."

"Good," the girl replied.

"What about our mom?" the second girl asked.

"I— I think I saw her body. I don't know what she looked like, so I can't say that for sure. There was a woman at the front door—"

Corn stalks snapped and dried leaves rattled off to his left. Jake spun, taking a knee and bringing his rifle up to his shoulder in a mostly coordinated motion. Three rows away, an infected was bulling through the field directly toward them.

The woman's warm breath on his neck startled him. "Don't shoot," she whispered, barely audible. "Just wait."

It went against everything Jake was trained to do. He'd always killed every infected he saw, thinking that each one killed was another step closer to ending this nightmare. But the girls had survived out here, outside of the walls of Fort Bliss, for seven months. Maybe they knew something that he didn't. He held his fire and watched the creature, ready to shoot it the moment it broke through the row in front of them.

It stopped. The male looked around and sniffed the air, trying to locate the humans it must have heard talking. Jake adjusted his aimpoint slightly, centering the IR laser attached to the rails of the M-4 on the center of its forehead.

It *knew* they were there, Jake was sure of it. Every fiber in his body screamed at him to kill it, end its miserable life and the immediate threat. The M-4 would make enough noise in this wide open, silent field to bring every infected within a mile directly to them. There was no telling how many more of them were in the field, and he estimated that he had about a hundred and fifty rounds left—plenty to go up against human targets like he'd planned, but not nearly enough for a running gunfight against a horde of infected coming from every direction.

The deranged scream of an infected pierced the night, making the creature in front of them snap its head in the opposite direction of the farmhouse. It hesitated for a moment and then took off running, screaming in response.

Jake breathed out slowly. He hadn't realized he'd been holding his breath. A soft pat on his shoulder reassured him that he'd done the right thing.

Somewhere nearby, probably less than three or four hundred meters, a horse cried out in terror. The sounds it made broke Jake's heart, but he knew that it was the best thing that could have happened for their survival. More infected joined the first, screaming as they streamed through the cornfield toward their meal.

They waited for a few minutes, then began the slow, arduous return trip to the safety of the Stryker. When they finally broke the edge of the field, they sprinted across the open gravel parking lot to the big vehicle. Jake opened the hatch and let the girls inside.

"I have to recover the bodies of my team," he told them, to which they nodded.

Neither girl said a word as he loaded Caitlyn's body into the back of the Stryker with them. He was respectful and took the time to wrap her in a blanket that one of the women who'd left El Paso with him had brought. It took a lot more dragging, pulling, and making noise to retrieve Dickerson's body. Jake was exhausted by the time he'd maneuvered the big man into the compartment.

When he was done, he used some wet wipes to clean away the blood from his hands. He showed the girls—he still wasn't sure which one was which—how to use the CVC helmets because he'd need their help navigating back to the Campbell farm.

Then he took off his body armor and crawled inside the driver's compartment to begin the trip back to the safety of the farm. With luck, they wouldn't run into any of the infected that were likely still streaming toward the scene from all over the countryside. The girls couldn't operate the machine gun up top—not that he'd want to risk more noise—so he'd have to try to run over anything he saw to keep them from following him back to the Campbell's place.

That, he could do, he thought, grinning as he gripped the Stryker's steering wheel, put it into gear, and pulled the big vehicle out of the farm's parking area. It didn't take long for his first target to appear, running down the dirt road, drawn by the sound of the big engines. He was already up to 30 miles per hour when the front slope of the Stryker clipped the infected at chest height. It went spinning off into the ditch, probably with several broken ribs and a cracked sternum.

He smiled and began to hum a tune to himself. In this crazy world, you had to find something to keep you from going insane yourself. Or maybe he was already certifiable. Maybe those were the only type of people who actually wanted to survive.

Jake was okay with that.

26

NEAR LIBERAL, KANSAS
DECEMBER 1ST

"How's mom and baby?" Vern asked, walking from the stove where he'd scooped a large helping of eggs from a pan onto his plate. He walked hunched and still required the assistance of a cane after his ordeal last month, but soon, he would be good to go and wouldn't have to rely so much on Jake and his granddaughters to keep up the farm.

"They're doing well," Carmen replied, adding a spoonful of scrambled eggs to her own plate. "Despite being about a month early, the baby seems extremely healthy, even full-term. I'd never say this to Sidney, but it makes me wonder if she was pregnant about a month *before* she thought she was."

"What? That's just— Never mind, none of my business. I wanna tell you what…" Vern began, pausing when Jake entered the dining room and set his rifle in the corner by the door. "Jake," he acknowledged.

"Mr. Campbell," the soldier inclined his head. "Sally's up in the lookout. Just gonna get some breakfast real quick, then head back up there."

Vern accepted it with a grunt. He was positive that Jake and Sally were sweet on each other— without any evidence, of course. It was just how they talked to one another, which could be attributed to their shared experiences at the Cullen farm, he guessed. If he looked at it truly objectively, as a Christian, then he knew that they were just friends, but given what he'd just been told by Carmen, he wasn't too sure about these city folks. The old man wanted to keep his grandchildren pure for when the *real* Army showed up eventually and took back the countryside.

Vern originally thought that Jake and Sidney were together and the baby was his. He couldn't keep these damn kids and their relationships straight. In reality, Jake and Carmen were the ones who were sweet on each other. They even slept in the same bedroom. He'd been opposed to it at first, but eventually relented. If Carmen kept the soldier honest with Sally and Katie, then he decided it was for the best.

Vern shook his head. "Now, what was I sayin'?"

"You asked about Sidney and baby Lincoln," Carmen replied, placing a hand over Jake's as he sat down beside her.

"Oh, that's right," he said. "I need to go congratulate that woman. I was worried that she'd be hollerin' something fierce. I remember when my Sarah had our boy, Jeff. Whoo wee! I think her screams were loud enough to rouse old Ezekiel's bones."

Carmen smiled, but Vern knew that she didn't understand the reference. She'd been raised Catholic and had almost no idea what the Old Testament said. But he was trying to work on that during their nightly bible study.

"She did very well," the nurse agreed. "She's probably one of the strongest women I've ever met during labor."

"Yeah, I thought we'd be shooting infected for days after today," Jake replied.

They'd taken extra precaution for the birth and ringed the house and the chicken coop with an additional layer of concertina wire. Turns out, they didn't need it. If Sidney had so much as whimpered during the baby's birth, Vern hadn't heard it.

"So, now that the baby's been born, what are you planning to do, Jake?" he asked, dreading the answer. The farm was a lot of work, even in the reduced capacity he'd been forced to operate at. Losing John, Scott, and Jesse was catastrophic for his and the girls' way of life. When he'd made the deal with the soldier on the day the girls were kidnapped, it had been with the understanding that their stay at the farm would be temporary.

"Well, sir," Jake replied after swallowing a mouthful of eggs. "If you'll have us, we'd like to stay on for a while. Not permanently, but just through the winter. Without Caitlyn and Dickerson's expertise at maintaining the Stryker, it'll be dangerous to drive in the winter."

Vern leaned back, taking in a sharp breath as his internal injuries sent a flash of pain through his body. He wasn't healed enough to work the farm exclusively. There was firewood to chop, cattle to feed, stalls to be cleaned out—all things the old man thought were too tough for the girls to do.

"Let me tell you, Jake. That makes me happy. I don't like to admit it, but until I heal up, I need your help around here."

"I know you do, Mr. Campbell," the soldier replied. "And we need your help. On the road, in the back of a Stryker, is no place for a newborn."

Vern reached his hand across the table, offering it to Jake. The younger man shook it. "Until spring then," the farmer stated.

"Until spring."

"Having that cat around will help with the mice," he grunted in acceptance of his new, long-term visitors. "Now, Miss Carmen." Vern looked at the woman. "You think Miss Sidney is ready for a visitor? I'd sure like to see that little feller before I go out to gather the eggs for the morning."

"I think that can be arranged," she replied. "If he's anything like his mother, he'll be tearing around this farm in no time."

Vern smiled knowingly. He'd made a deal with Jake, but he knew they were here for the long run, until this plague ran its course, or the Good Lord came back, whichever came first.

EPILOGUE

"I want those deserters found. Immediately. Do I make myself clear, Jim?"

Jim Albrecht scratched idly at his shoulder where the wound from the uprising two months ago was finally starting to heal. Doctors assured him that with time, he might even be able to raise his left arm above his head. "Might" being the key word in their prognosis.

"Sir, what good does it do us to go after Lieutenant Murphy?"

"Watch yourself, Colonel," Major General Bhagat cautioned. "I will not allow a lieutenant to incite a riot—check that. To cause an outright rebellion. The person who started all of this isn't just going to get away free and clear. I want him brought to justice."

Jim tempered his response. The uprising would have happened whether Jake Murphy was at the camp or not. That had been the general's plan all along. He wanted a small-scale revolt that would eliminate a hundred thousand refugees. That would have bought them a few more months' worth of food, enough time for the second site at Yuma Proving Grounds to be completed.

But the carnage that'd ensued during the rebellion was on an unforeseen scale. Almost all of Camp Three was in ruins. The close confines of the base walls made it like shooting fish in a barrel for both sides. Hundreds of thousands of refugees were dead or dying, an entire brigade—*his* brigade—was combat ineffective due to death and injuries, and an untold amount of food had been destroyed when the refugees set fire to the warehouses before the threat was finally eliminated.

The general's little revolt was a nightmare that the men and women of the First Armored Division had to live with on a daily basis.

"Sir, that rebellion would have occurred whether Murphy was there or not," Jim countered. "It was a powder keg, waiting to explode."

The division commander held up his hand. "Just stop right there, Jim. I won't let you defend that piece of garbage deserter. My S-6 tells me that his Stryker's BFT pinged up at some small town in Oklahoma called Tyrone about a month ago. Since then it's been turned off or destroyed, we don't know which."

He sighed and stood before continuing. "It's a nasty business, Jim. But I can't let the Iron soldiers think they can desert their unit without consequences. Now, are you gonna go get my Stryker back or do I need to find a new Ready Six?"

There it is, then, Jim thought to himself. The old man was threatening to shitcan him if he didn't go after Murphy. Given their current state of affairs, he didn't have the luxury of retiring and fading away when morally ambiguous circumstances arose like his predecessors had. He would remain on Fort Bliss until the siege was over. He couldn't put himself—or his family—through that.

"I can put together about a platoon of men, sir," Jim Albrecht stated. "Can't guarantee any more than that."

The general smiled. "I knew I could count on you, Jim. Now go drag that worthless deserter back here so he can face a military tribunal."

Jim stood quickly, his shoulder protesting the movement as he brought up his other arm in a stiff salute. "Yes, sir," he said.

The general returned it, seemingly annoyed at the protocol that everyone still followed. "Dismissed, Jim. Now that this business with the uprising is over, I have to prepare a report for the president."

Jim nodded and turned to leave. He sure as hell wasn't looking forward to the upcoming mission. But he had a job to do, and by God, he was going to get it done.

This is the end of the first installment of Sidney's Way. Her story will continue shortly.

The Five Roads to Texas world is ever expanding. Look for more adventures from the minds of other Phalanx Press authors soon.

ABOUT THE AUTHOR

A veteran of the wars in Iraq and Afghanistan, Brian Parker was born and raised as an Army brat. He's currently an Active Duty Army soldier who enjoys spending time with his family in Texas, hiking, obstacle course racing, writing and Texas Longhorns football. He's an unashamed Star Wars fan, but prefers to disregard the entire Episode I and II debacle.

Brian is both a traditionally- and self-published author with an ever-growing collection of works across multiple genres, including sci-fi, post-apocalyptic, horror, paranormal thriller, military fiction, self-publishing how-to and even a children's picture book, *Zombie in the Basement*, which he wrote to help children overcome the perceived stigma of being different from others.

He is also the founder of Muddy Boots Press, an independent publishing company that focuses on quality genre fiction over mass-produced books.

FOLLOW BRIAN ON SOCIAL MEDIA!

Facebook: www.facebook.com/BrianParkerAuthor
Twitter: www.twitter.com/BParker_Author

OTHER AUTHORS UNDER THE SHIELD OF

SIXTH CYCLE

Nuclear war has destroyed human civilization.
Captain Jake Phillips wakes into a dangerous new world, where he finds the remaining fragments of the population living in a series of strongholds, connected across the country. Uneasy alliances have maintained their safety, but things are about to change. -- Discovery leads to danger. -- Skye Reed, a tracker from the Omega stronghold, uncovers a threat that could spell the end for their fragile society. With friends and enemies revealing truths about the past, she will need to decide who to trust. -- **Sixth Cycle** is a gritty post-apocalyptic story of survival and adventure.

Darren Wearmouth ~ Carl Sinclair

The Invasion Trilogy

Aliens have planned against us for centuries... And now the attack is ready.

Charlie Jackson's archaeological team find advanced technology in an undisturbed 16th Century graves. While investigating the discovery, giant sinkholes appear across planet, marking the start of Earth's colonization and the descent of civilization.

Charlie and the rest of humanity will have to fight for survival, sacrificing the life they've known to protect themselves from an ancient and previously dormant enemy. Even that might not be enough as aliens exact a plan that will change the course of history.

Darren Wearmouth

DEAD ISLAND: Operation Zulu

Ten years after the world was nearly brought to its knees by a zombie Armageddon, there is a race for the antidote! On a remote Caribbean island, surrounded by a horde of hungry living dead, a team of American and Australian commandos must rescue the Antidotes' scientist. Filled with zombies, guns, Russian bad guys, shady government types, serial killers and elevator muzak. Dead Island is an action packed blood soaked horror adventure.
Dead Island: Dos and ***Dead Island: Ravenous*** are available now!

Allen Gamboa

INVASION OF THE DEAD SERIES

This is the first book in a series of nine, about an ordinary bunch of friends, and their plight to survive an apocalypse in Australia. -- Deep beneath defense headquarters in the Australian Capital Territory, the last ranking Army chief and a brilliant scientist struggle with answers to the collapse of the world, and the aftermath of an unprecedented virus. Is it a natural mutation, or does the infection contain -- more sinister roots? -- One hundred and fifty miles away, five friends returning from a month-long camping trip slowly discover that death has swept through the country. What greets them in a gradual revelation is an enemy beyond compare. -- Armed with dwindling ammunition, the friends must overcome their disagreements, utilize their individual skills, and face unimaginable horrors as they battle to reach their hometown.

Owen Baillie

Whiskey Tango Foxtrot

Alone in a foreign land. The radio goes quiet while on convoy in Afghanistan, a lost patrol alone in the desert. With his unit and his home base destroyed, Staff Sergeant Brad Thompson suddenly finds himself isolated and in command of a small group of men trying to survive in the Afghan wasteland. Every turn leads to danger.
The local population has been afflicted with an illness that turns them into rabid animals. They pursue him and his men at every corner and stop. Struggling to hold his team together and unite survivors, he must fight and evade his way to safety. A fast paced zombie war story like no other.

W.J. Lundy

ZOMBIE RUSH

New to the Hot Springs PD Lisa Reynolds was not all that welcomed by her coworkers especially those who were passed over for the position. It didn't matter, her thirty days probation ended on the same day of the Z-poc's arrival. Overnight the world goes from bad to worse as thousands die in the initial onslaught. National Guard and regular military unit deployed the day before to the north leaves the city in mayhem. All directions lead to death until one unlikely candidate steps forward with a plan. A plan that became an avalanche raging down the mountain culminating in the salvation or destruction of them all.

Joseph Hansen

ZED'S WORLD
BOOK ONE: THE GATHERING HORDE
The most ambitious terrorist plot ever undertaken is about to be put into motion, releasing an unstoppable force against humanity. Ordinary people – A group of students celebrating the end of the semester, suburban and rural families – are about to themselves in the center of something that threatens the survival of the human species. As they battle the dead – and the living – it's going to take every bit of skill, knowledge and luck for them to survive in Zed's World.

BOOK TWO: ROADS LESS TRAVELED
A terrible plague has been loosed upon the earth. In the course of one night, mankind teeters on the brink of extinction. Fighting through gathering hordes of undead, a group of friends brave military checkpoints, armed civilians, and forced allegiances in an attempt to reach loved ones. Thwarted at every turn, they press forward. But taking roads less traveled, could cost them everything.

BOOK THREE: NO WAY OUT
For Kyle Puckett, Earth has become a savage place. As the world continues to decay, the survivors of the viral plague have started choosing sides. With each encounter the stakes - and the body count - continue to rise. With the skies growing darker and the dead pressing in, both sides may soon find out that there is No Way Out.

Rich Baker

Grudge
The United States Navy led an expedition to Antarctica in December 1946, called Operation Highjump. Officially, the men were tasked with evaluating the effect of cold weather on US equipment; secretly their mission was to investigate reports of a hidden Nazi base buried beneath the ice. After engaging unknown forces in aerial combat, weather forced the Navy to abandon operations. Undeterred, the US returned every Antarctic summer until finally the government detonated three nuclear missiles over the atmosphere in 1958. Unfortunately, the desperate gamble to rid the world of the Nazi scourge failed. The enemy burrowed deeper into the ice, using alien technologies for cryogenic freezing to amass a genetically superior army, indoctrinated from birth to hate Americans. Now they've returned, intent on exacting revenge for the destruction of their homeland and banishment to the icy wastes.

The Path of Ashes

Evil doesn't become extinct, it evolves. Our world is a violent place. Murder, terrorism, racism and social inequality, these are some of the forces that attempt to destroy our society while the State is forced to increase its response to these actions. Our own annihilation is barely held at bay by the belief that we've somehow evolved beyond our ancestors' base desires.

From this cesspool of emotions emerges a madman, intent on leading the world into anarchy. When his group of computer hackers infiltrate the Department of Defense network, they initiate a nuclear war that will irrevocably alter our world.

Aeric Gaines and his roommate, Tyler, survive the devastation of the war, only to find that the politically correct world where they'd been raised was a lie. All humans have basic needs such as food, water and shelter…but we will fight for what we *desire*.

A Path of Ashes is a three-book series about life in post-apocalyptic America, a nation devoid of leadership, electricity and human rights. The world as we know it may have burned, but humanity found a way to survive and this is their story.

Brian Parker

Human Element

The Neuroweb began as the greatest invention since written language. A simple brain implant that allowed the user to access information, entertainment, and even pain relief. The Neuroweb was the beginning of a golden age for mankind…

Until it was compromised.

Everyone with the implant lost their most important commodity: their free will. The collective human consciousness was hacked, and now directed by artificial intelligence. Only those without the Neuroweb have a chance of resisting…If they dare.

Aaran has legitimate reason to believe he's the last free-thinking human alive. After his family was killed in the purge, he fled for his life. Now, he aimlessly wanders through the suburbs of Cincinnati alone, desperate to find a reason to live.

When he meets a girl like him - another free thinker - they search together for a cause worth fighting for. Worth dying for.

As the Ash Fell

Life in the frozen wastelands of Texas is anything but easy, but for Clay Whitaker there is always more at stake than mere survival.

It's been seven years since the ash billowed into the atmosphere, triggering some of the harshest winters in recorded history. Populations are thinning. Food is scarce. Despair overwhelming. With no way to sustain order, societies collapsed, leaving people to fend for themselves.

Clay and his sister Megan have taken a handful of orphaned children into their home--a home soaring sixteen stories into the sky. With roughly six short months a year to gather enough food and supplies to last the long, brutal winter, Clay must spend most of his time away from his family to scavenge, hunt, and barter.

When Clay rescues a young woman named Kelsey from a group of Screamers, his life is catapulted into a new direction, forcing him to make decisions he never thought he would have to make.

Now, with winter rolling in earlier than ever, Clay's divided attention is putting him, and his family, at risk.

AJ Powers

Printed in Poland
by Amazon Fulfillment
Poland Sp. z o.o., Wrocław